Café Bombshell

The International Brain Surgery Conspiracy

Published and Forthcoming by New Academia Publishing

SCARITH Books
Fiction / Poetry

Pets of the Great Dictators & Other Works, by Sabrina P. Ramet

Always the Trains, by Judy Neri

Brothers in Exile: A Novel of the Lives and Loves of Thomas and Heinrich Mann, by Selig Kainer

Love and Samsāra, by Eusebio L. Rodrigues

Sons, by Jonathan Kleinbard

Out of What Chaos, by Lee Oser

The Da Vinci Barcode: A Parody, by Judith P. Shoaf

On the Way to Red Square, by Julieta Almeida Rodrigues

New Academia Books
Literature: Theory and Criticism

Russian Futurism: A History, by Vladimir Markov

Words in Revolution: Russian Futurist Manifestoes 1912-1928
A. Lawton and H. Eagle, eds., trs.

Shakespeare's Theater of Likeness, by R. Allen Shoaf

Living Novels: A Journey through Twentieth-Century Fiction
by Sascha Talmor

On the Road to Baghdad, or Traveling Biculturalism: Theorizing a Bicultural Approach to Contemporary World Fiction
Gönul Pultar, ed.

To read an excerpt, visit www.newacademia.com

Café Bombshell

The International
Brain Surgery Conspiracy

Sabrina P. Ramet

SCARITH

An imprint of New Academia Publishing
Washington, DC

New Academia Publishing, 2008

Library of Congress Control Number: 2008925066
ISBN 978-0-9800814-8-0 paperback (alk. paper)

New Academia Publishing, LLC
P.O. Box 27420 - Washington, DC 20038-7420
www.newacademia.com - info@newacademia.com

For John, Tetsuo, Shin and Tomoko, Osamu, Rihito and Yuki, Lea and Miro, and Shepilov who joined them (OK, maybe he didn't) and for the brain surgeons of Sapporo and Kyoto

Contents

Preface

Most of the action taking place in this story occurred in the mid-1980s, when the threat of industrial pollution was already well known. I was perhaps one of the first to realize that industrial pollution was interconnected with a vast international conspiracy of brain surgeons. I found evidence of this conspiracy not only in the proliferation of brain surgery clinics and in their activities, but in coded messages embedded in bus schedules, in syringe marks on fruit, even in television commercials. Although I played only a minor role in the struggle against the brain surgeons, I felt it was my duty as a living being to record these strange events exactly as they occurred, so that the truth could be known.

Bill Mongoose

1

Mind Control and How to Fight it

I knew it was going to be a good day when Astrolabe, my fuzzy Persian, didn't mess all over the kitchen floor. Usually she messes all over the floor, not in her kitty litter, and I gotta clean it all up. Not at all like Sextant, our hermaphrodite Siamese cat, who always knows where to mess. But today Astrolabe messed in her litter, and when I saw that, I said to myself, Hey, this is going to be a good day. And I was right. Usually the cat messes all over the floor, as if she can't make it to the litter box. And then when I get up in the morning, the whole place stinks and I have to clean it up. Kris says that Sextant -- we call her Sexy for short -- is *her* cat, and Astrolabe is *my* cat. I don't remember the justification for this division, but it means that I am responsible for cleaning up

Astrolabe's mess. So every morning, before I go to work, I put on the 1935 recording of "Also Sprach Zarathustra" that Serge Koussevitzky made with the Boston Symphony, and wash the kitchen floor. I usually have to wash the floor again when I get home from work, because Astrolabe usually misses the target. But that particular morning was different. And the cat hadn't even died. Here, she was still alive and had done her business in the litter box.

I've been reading about all of this mind control stuff. Now they made some computer chip that replicates your brain cells, so who needs an organic brain anymore? They implant these chips in people's brains when they go in for a routine physical or an X-ray or even for an eye exam. I understand that even some barbers are in on it. It's mind control, that's what it is. And now all these lobotomies! Lobotomy is serious business. You shouldn't go and get a lobotomy unless you think about it first, because you're not going to be in any shape to think about it afterwards. Of course, a lot of it is involuntary. I just hope I can get out before they come after me.

But I knew they wouldn't come that day, because the cat didn't mess on the floor. That was a good start. I didn't have to clean the floor that morning. The people at the supermarket would ask me why I was buying so much floorcleaner. I just told them that I like to keep my floors clean as a whistle. They joked with me, all in good fun, said I must be cleaning floors on the side and maybe I would like to come over to their houses and clean their floors too, but I told them, No, I've already got a job. Professor of History at the University of Washington.

So I had extra time on my hands what with not having to clean the floor, and so I decided to stop by Union Station and check the departures. Got to keep alert. Never know when you might want to make a break for it and get out. Go to Mexico or something. And you can't trust the airlines, what with all their crashes. I mean, Seattle is going to the dogs, the final crash might come very suddenly and it'll be a scramble then. Best to know what the train schedules are. 6:30 a.m. for Portland, continuing on to Boise. 8:46 a.m. for Portland, continuing on to Los Angeles and Ensenada, Mexico. 9:15 a.m. express train to Phoenix. 10:20 a.m. to Vancouver. 11:23 a.m. for Calgary. That's one place I don't ever want to go.

I cut my own hair. That started about three years ago when I found out what was going on in these so-called "barber shops". I remember one place where I was having a nice conversation with the barber and heard plenty of snipping sounds, and was remarking to myself how neat the barber was, not letting any snipped hair fall onto my lap. Then I got up for a moment and tripped over an electrical cord. In a flash, the "barber" disappeared. He had only been a hologram. That made me think. Then I tried the competition. Had a very striking name: "the First National Barber Shop". It was a bank-owned financial front organization. At least *their* barbers actually cut the hair, but they seemed a bit scatter-brained, had too many standardized replies. They would say, "Good morning, have a seat, we'll be right with you" every time the door opened, even if it was because someone was leaving. I realized that these "barbers" were actually audio-animatronic robots. No doubt working far below minimum wage.

Mind control takes many forms. Subliminal messages on television and e-mail, product promotion in films, and this constant soothing prattle on the news programs trying to put us all into a state of blissful equanimity. They want us to believe that all we have to worry about is murder, rape, arson, robbery, invasion, impoverishment, car crashes, pestilence, AIDS, riots, earthquakes, floods, sudden loss of electricity, sudden loss of memory, Alzheimer's disease, strikes by bus drivers, corruption, juvenile delinquency, the subversion of the legal system, terrorism, global warming, alien abductions, and the growing gulf between the rich and the poor. Life should be so simple! No, the reality is, as I have learned, far more complex, far more disturbing. So you have to be careful. Very careful. Otherwise, who knows, you could lose your mind.

Take the case of prozac. People say it makes them feel sanguine and content. Jolly, I call it. But it's not healthy to be so jolly. You start to accept everything they tell you. The coffee houses are dens of prozac. Take, for example, Queequeg's -- Seattle's most popular coffee house chain. Why do you think everyone looks so jolly at Queequeg's? Then, while they have their customers in so receptive and vulnerable a disposition, they feed them subliminal messages in the musac. Seattle wants to be the Republic of Latte. Well, count me out!

Some handy rules: Avoid juices of all kinds, especially from concentrates. Check all fruit and vegetables for syringe marks. Avoid grapes altogether. Where crackers are concerned, eat only Finnish crackers. Avoid ground meats of all kinds. Eat only imported butter. And *never* buy large, bargain sizes. One can never be too careful.

That's one of the reasons I like the old recordings. They were made before they started putting all those subliminal messages into the tracks. So you can listen to Willem Mengelberg's 1928 recording of "Ein Heldenleben" with the New York Philharmonic without fear. They haven't gotten around to "fixing" it yet. I have proof.

Kris, my wife of six years, had been in the Resistance for many years. Fought with the Mannequin Liberation Front. Tied herself to Trident missiles in some sort of protest. I forget the details. On one occasion, she even traveled to Iran, back in the days of the Shah, and became involved in international subversion. Then one day she decided to go straight, went on a diet, started using makeup, threw away all her fatigues and filled her closet with leather skirts, silk blouses, and taffeta gowns. Now she likes to fix pretty bows in her hair and keeps the house very very tidy. *Very* tidy.

I've tried a couple of times to talk to Kris about her years with the Resistance. But whenever I've tried, she always turns the conversation to cleaning, and usually starts cleaning something.

She's not so worried about lobotomies as I am, although she appreciates the risk. She says that nobody in her family has ever had a lobotomy. I'm not sure what that has to do with anything. How is it that after all those years in the Resistance, she has no sense of the importance of self-defense, of protection? Maybe she's forgotten.

I hate elevators. Being trapped like that without any possibility of escape. And then they get inside with you. Of course they want you to think they just happen to be in the same elevator. They don't want you to realize that they've been following you. But they can't fool me. They want to control me. They want to take out my brain, so that they can continue with their skulduggery. Better to take the stairs.

We voted differently in the election. The party bosses wanted us to choose between Mondale and Reagan, but I thought about it and it seemed to me that the best president we had ever had was Franklin Delano Roosevelt. So I wrote in his name for president. I figured so what if he was dead. He knew how to pick good advisers and I figured that his advisers wouldn't be dead. Kris said that I had wasted my vote. But Kris had trouble choosing between the two major party candidates, because both of them dressed neatly and washed their hands regularly. So she decided to vote for both of them. I told her that her ballot would be thrown out and that she had wasted her vote. But she said that it felt good to vote for men who were neat and clean. At any rate, Reagan was back in office as our president and I just hoped that he understood the danger that the international brain surgery conspiracy represented.

2

Arc of Splendour

Before our stint in Japan, we lived in the Green Lake district of Seattle in a split-level house. We had picked it out because we wanted to be within walking distance of the lake. I guess at one time there must have been something green there. But by the time we moved into the area, it was well on the way to being renamed Yellow Lake, after the rancid yellow mist that floated above the putrescent waters of this industrial toxic cess pool. I understand that there used to be some park areas around the lake, and that people actually walked around the lake for exercise. But by the time we moved into the area, most of the lakefront areas had been taken up by industrial plants, such as Green Lake Machine Parts, Finster Chemicals, the Hydropak Tire Company, and the Arc of Splendour Glue Factory.

Finster Street runs parallel to the lake and many commercial enterprises have been built along Finster Street, serving various needs and wants. At the time we lived there, the familiar Queequeg's occupied the corner position at the southern end of the street, its mug-shaped turrets casting a shadow on Mistress Zorka's massage parlor. Next to the massage parlor was the Convent of St. Serena of the Seven Sorrowful Psychiatrists. The convent was run by Sister Drusilla, Mother Superior, and her assistant (Mother Inferior), Sister Flora Simea. The sisters did many good works in the area, especially resuscitating people who fainted from hydrocarbon inhalation and ministering to people and animals ailing from other pollution-induced afflictions ranging from hallucinations to temporary involuntary invisibility. The convent shared the block with three more installations: an exercise lounge with big windows, where beautiful people could show off their beauty; a tanning salon with connecting doors to a funeral parlour (both run by the same man); and the secret headquarters of a clandestine paramilitary unit led by Svetozar Umrovich (I wish I knew what they were up to).

The other side of Finster Street was dominated by the Green Lake Glue Factory and several surveillance facilities: the Telephone Tapping Agency, the Mail Inspection Center, and the E-Mail Surveillance Center. There was also a facility next to them called the National Encoding Corporation. I'd wanted to go in and ask them what they do, but I was afraid to do so. They might have turned me over to the glue factory -- or worse yet, to the Arc of Splendour Brain Surgery Clinic also on the same block.

There was just one more facility on the block -- the Arc of Splendour Glow Works, an olde English Shoppe that sold items that glowed: fluorescent rocks, fluorescent paint, fluorescent soap, fluorescent cheese, fluorescent shirts, fluorescent wine, and so forth.

I guess I worry about the Arc of Splendour. It's probably a multinational corporation, but I checked in the library and couldn't find any evidence that the Arc of Splendour had been registered either in Seattle or anywhere else.

I always woke up at 4 a.m. in those days, in order to check on the prematitudinal activities of these facilities. All of their subversive activities transpired between 4 a.m. and 7 a.m., leaving me plenty of time to clean up Astrolabe's mess before going to the office. Some of these activities were just not normal. For example, every morning I saw a van arrive at the Glue Factory and men in grey overalls carrying in caged peacocks, frogs, sheep, goats, and ravens, not to mention various endangered species.

Arc of Splendour also made candies and soft drinks. They bought the run-off from the Glue Factory and some of the other plants and made candy out of pollution. If you went to Arc of Splendour Fine Treats you could get a bag of sulfodiosweets and a nitrobar (manufactured from nitrogen oxides), and wash it down with a can of sulfo cola or carbonomonade. They even had a cereal: PBT flakes. Some people claimed to like these treats, but I saw a lot of these people crawling into the convent complaining of respiratory problems, headaches, dizziness, vomiting, temporary blindness, and even temporary insanity. They even advertised how they manufactured these deadly treats. Their motto: Today's waste -- tomorrow's taste!

They don't tell us the truth. And so the one thing you can rely upon is that nothing does what it's "supposed" to. On the contrary, most things in society work *opposite* to what their stated purpose is, and *this is by design*. "There are no accidents, no flaws in the design." I think it was Nietzsche who said that.

I've heard that somewhere in the neighborhood there was something called the Mirinda Out-of-Body Travel Service. Someone once showed me a brochure. It read:

"Mirinda Out-of-Body Travel Service
— Slash your travel expenses.

— Eliminate air fares.

— Eliminate expensive hotel accommodations.

—Try our out-of-body experiences. We can put you over there while your body is still on our gurney. Low prices. Special group rates.

You won't need to pay the fare,
Send your mind anywhere."

The only question is: what do they do to your brain while your mind is out having a nice time?

When we first moved to Green Lake, we shared the house with two young men -- Moe and Bo – who lived on the lower level of the split-level house. I think they were related in some way, but I was never able to determine just how. Moe seemed to give the orders, even though he had a rather suspicious-looking scar running from ear to ear right above the brow line. Bo, on the other hand, was the charmer -- sweet, pleasant, gentle, almost feminine in his ways. His main problem was that he was usually drunk. Although there were two clearly identifiable trash cans in the rear of the house, for our common use, their idea of dumping trash was throwing it somewhere in the vicinity of the trash cans. Kris, who always repeats that cleanliness is next to godliness, would always rush to clean up their mess until I decided that Moe and Bo should clean it up for themselves. And they did so. It was about that time, however, that they started borrowing money from us on a regular basis. "We're not a bank," I told them.

All of this might have been sufferable but for the advanced state of decay into which the house was rapidly sliding. The most immediately obvious problem was the fence around the yard, which sagged at a 45-degree angle. But there were other problems ranging from dead sockets throughout the house to a laundry room with dead washing machines and a leaky roof. But the worst of it was the heating system. Just to look at it you would have thought that everything was completely normal: a thermostat that you could set wherever you liked, and heating vents from which one might expect heat to emanate. So much for theory. In practice, the heating system shut down automatically every three hours or so, and could only be restarted at the master control panel located in the apartment below us; so, if Moe and Bo were sleeping or out or simply not in the mood, we wouldn't get any heat. After experiencing several evenings of 25—30 degree temperatures, we decided that maybe we *were* a bank.

As I mentioned, most of the action in our neighborhood took place between 4 a.m. and 7 a.m. But there was one facility where there was almost always something to see: Happy Harry's Tanning Salon and Funeral Parlour. His establishment was emblazoned with a gaily painted sign: "Get a tan while we prepare your loved ones for burial!" Happy Harry deserved his name. I often saw him standing in front of his business grinning ear to ear, with a glazed look in his eyes. Happy Harry would bounce around his shop -- you couldn't call it walking -- and generally looked like he was having the time of his life. It's always nice when people enjoy their work.

3

Zeko: an Introduction

I first met Zeko in Bartell Drugs on 45th Street a few years ago, after we had been living above Moe and Bo for about a year. I wanted to buy a stuffed rabbit. It was near Easter. So there were lots of stuffed rabbits at Bartell's. They were lined up on the shelf like fresh recruits just out of basic training. I picked out a particularly fuzzy model with big floppy ears. She was dressed in combat fatigues and identified as "Stuffed Rabbit, Eco-terrorist model". As I bent over to take a closer look at her, I thought I heard the word "Zeko" being whispered into my ear. I turned around and didn't see anyone, perhaps I was just imagining it. But the word sounded like a name, and so I decided to call this "Eco-terrorist model" Zeko.

Did I take Zeko home with me or did she follow me? I'm no longer entirely sure. But whatever the case, upon arriving home, I immediately showed her to Kris.

"Oh that's nice, Bill darling," said Kris, without paying too much attention. "Why don't you put it on the bed for decoration?"

I tossed Zeko onto the pillow, then adjusted her so that she faced toward the foot of the bed. Of course, Kris rushed over and readjusted Zeko, seeming to be intent on placing her equidistant from the two edges.

At first Zeko seemed to be just an ordinary stuffed rabbit. She just sat around with a totally vacant look on her face and didn't say anything. Even her whiskers were motionless.

The first sign of life in her came about three weeks after we purchased her, when I was making the bed. I tossed Zeko from one side of the bed to the other as I worked. When I was finished, I triumphantly plopped her on the pillow. As I did so, I thought I saw a gleam in her eye. That gleam must mean something, I thought, but I was too slow-witted to know what. But she was clearly looking at me. She could see me. I felt she was thinking something and I didn't know what.

Her first words came a few minutes later, and rather shocked me. I still remember them. Kris and I were in the front room. We had brought Zeko out with us and had set her on the coffee table. Suddenly we heard a very high-pitched female voice ring out.

"Where are my explosives?"

Kris and I looked at each other in puzzlement. The voice continued.

"I said, *where* are my explosives?!"

We were dumb-founded and confused. The high-pitched voice grew impatient.

"You two look like a couple of dumb bunnies just sitting there as if you'd never heard a rabbit talk before! What's wrong with you two?"

"Huh?" we mumbled.

"Look, I have some important business to attend to." This was to be a recurrent refrain with Zeko. "And I don't have any time to waste. I had some high-tech explosives with me. There are megacorporations out there which are destroying natural habitats and industrial polluters wrecking the environment. I need to blow them up! Now, where are my explosives? Where did you put them? I have to go out and save the planet!"

Kris and I had recovered our senses, at least to some extent, by now. "This isn't happening," Kris said to herself, looking somewhat distracted.

"You're talking, Zeko. How is this possible?" I asked.

"We can talk about rabbit anatomy later," replied Zeko. "Right now I have to save Wallingford from a wave of industrial waste being pumped into the water main and to do that I need to demolish the factory – and I *have to get moving!* Why, it's already 1:47!"

"I don't know anything about your explosives, Zeko," I answered firmly but calmly.

"Look, Comrade," Zeko replied. Hereafter, this was the only name by which Zeko ever addressed me. "If you didn't hide my explosives, then maybe Kris did."

Kris was not reachable, however. She just kept repeating to herself, "This isn't happening, this isn't real. Wake up, Kris, wake up. Oh, it's no good, I can't wake up."

"You can't go around confiscating other people's explosives."

"But we didn't –"

"How would you like it if I confiscated your furniture?"

"But you're only a stuffed rabbit!"

"And you are only a human. So what?!" Zeko grunted with increasing exasperation. "OK, let's compromise. If you take me shopping and buy me a new arsenal and a truckload of grenades, I'll forget all about the fact that Kris confiscated my explosives and weaponry. We'll just let by-gones be by-gones."

Kris left the room about this time, so she couldn't answer this renewed charge. I heard her gargling in the bathroom. How was gargling going to help, I wondered.

I decided to play along. "What kind of explosives and weapons do you need, Zeko?"

"Now you're talking, Comrade," Zeko said, beaming. "I need about 30 rocket-launchers for the time being, maybe four mortars, also some hand-held anti-tank weapons, maybe half a dozen surface-to-surface missiles, and an equal number of surface-to-air missiles, and I'll need a helicopter, and about five tons of explosives, and also maybe 50 M-16s. That would be useful. OK?" Zeko smiled winningly.

"I'll just call up my friend, President Assad, and see what he can do," I said (in jest).

"You know Hafez!" Zeko seemed impressed.

"No, Zeko," I said in a serious tone of voice. "I don't, and I can't get you this kind of weaponry. This is incredible. What do you want to do, blow up Jamaica?"

"No. I am an eco-terrorist, a defender of the planet, and I need these explosives to fight the polluters and land developers," Zeko answered.

"Yes, I know," I sighed, not sure whether I should be as concerned as I was starting to feel.

"Kris," I said later, after Zeko had given up and had gone off to sulk and sleep it off, "I think we have a rabbit eco-terrorist on our hands. She's some sort of green anarchist, I guess."

Kris was busy dusting the tops of all of our doors, but she listened with attention. But even now Kris took some convincing. But finally she started to take it seriously and asked, "OK, what do we do? Report Zeko to the FBI?"

"Well, there's a problem with that," I admitted. "First of all, she may be working for the FBI – in which case reporting her wouldn't make any sense. And if she isn't working for the FBI, then let's say that the authorities come to arrest her. But

Zeko is very smart. She knows how to look very inanimate. The police will take one look at her and figure that we're nuts. And then we end up going in for psychiatric evaluation."

"Then we have no choice but to cover for Zeko, I guess," Kris said, although I could see she was not too happy about this conclusion. "Our house is being converted, without our agreement, into a center the defense of the planet. It sounds dangerous. Maybe we can wean her away from her present line of work..."

"Of course, it's always possible that Zeko is suffering from delusions of grandeur, and that she only imagines that she is some sort of heroic fighter against corporate polluters," I said. "After all, we don't have any evidence of any bold exploits."

"How old is she anyway, Bill darling?" Kris asked.

"Well, it didn't say on her label. It only said that she was manufactured in Thailand and registered in Ohio, Maine, and Massachusetts."

"What if we call the Thai embassy?" Kris wondered out loud.

"And say what? Ask them if their stuffed animals are equipped with artificial intelligence units?"

"Yeah, something like that."

We didn't come to any big conclusions that day, but at least Zeko was quiet for the time being. Trying to be careful not to wake up our irrepressible new companion, we sneaked out of the house and took dinner out, at one of the restaurants facing Lake Union. There we tried to get our minds off Zeko.

4

Zeko's Career as a Secret Agent

"So what are *you* doing to save the planet?" Zeko asked me the following morning.

"I keep up to date with train schedules," I answered, "and I avoid brain surgery clinics," although I was still not quite sure whether I should be talking to my stuffed rabbit.

"Well, that's not much of a contribution, is it?" Zeko replied.

"OK, Zeko, I'm sure you're right," I replied. "But what's all this about blowing up things? And what were you doing on the shelf of Bartell's, if you're a trained eco-terrorist."

"Oh yes, about that," Zeko seemed very pleased with herself. "Our unit came up with this idea, actually it was my idea, since I am the unit commander. We decided that the best way to further our objectives was to infiltrate ordinary homes like yours, which are on the front line of the defense, and the easiest way was to sit on the shelf and let you pay to take us with you. Of course, it did bring back some unfortunate memories of being held for ransom, but that couldn't be avoided."

Zeko was anything but reticent about her background and career. In the succeeding weeks we were treated to a seemingly endless series of stories of various acts of apparent bravery, mostly involving paw-to-hand combat with polluters and their underpaid employees, swinging from ropes at great heights, leaping over blazing vehicles, and foiling corporate capers of various sorts, ostensibly often involving the use of explosives. Our stuffed rabbit, it turned out, had obtained some sort of advanced training a few years earlier, at Fort Bragg, when she was apparently thinking of working as a government secret agent. Then she defected to the anarchists, and, in the quest for terrorist training, spent time at two of Libya's top training camps. There, in Libya, under the guidance of North Korean, East German, and Palestinian instructors, she had learned the techniques of "reception" and deception. She also became one of the top specialists in bridge demolition. She was decorated with the Order of the Camel by Muammar al-Qaddafi himself. She had consorted with the infamous Carlos the Jackal, not otherwise associated with bridges. She had been friends with Hafez and Yasir back in the early days even before they signed treaties of friendship with the Soviet Union and started making these visits to Moscow where they would kiss Brezhnev and his friends. She was apparently so successful in winning the trust of the Libyans and that she had even been given command of a mysterious training camp at Ben-Azir for about two years. Since then, she had taken to calling herself "commander."

Judging from her stories, 'Commander Zeko' had waged a 'one-rabbit' war against the forces of evil and disorder, and had left behind a monumental trail of carrot stubs. (She was apparently a carrot addict of sorts.) She claimed to have destroyed half a dozen pollutant plants in Germany, the same number in France, three in Greece, four in England, one in Luxembourg, and 16 across the United States, concentrating her efforts, according to her account, in Georgia and Alabama, before moving to Seattle. Did she have any regrets about choosing this line of work? Only one, evidently: that she had up to then not been able to perfect a plan to use the underwater "chunnel" linking Britain and the Continent for any televizable exploits.

Zeko seemed to know a lot about bridges. She had evidently studied this subject quite closely. She could tell you what building materials were used, in what quantities, for different bridges, where their points of stress were, how much sag was normal, and, of course, which were the best places to situate your explosives for maximum effect. I guess she must have had a lot of hot pursuits over bridges.

I bought Zeko some books about bridges, including a lovely picture book devoted entirely to the enormous suspension bridge in Sydney.

"Oooh," Zeko cooed with such delight that I half-expected her to start purring like a cat. But of course, rabbits don't purr; rabbits aren't cats.

"Oooh, I would love to blow up that bridge," she said, as she fondled a blow-up showing some of the bridge's principal beams, "but of course it would need to be in the course of making my escape from the corporate exploiters."

As long as I kept supplying Zeko with books about bridges, she seemed content to study them and to gaze longingly at the pictures, although I did notice that, from time to time, she jotted down some notes in a small notebook. But she seemed, at least for the time being, to forget about her work as an eco-terrorist. I bought her beautiful picture books about Tower Bridge in London, about Golden Gate

Bridge, about the Mendota bridge connecting St. Paul to the rest of civilization, the Lion Bridge in Budapest, the Tsing Ma Bridge in Hong Kong, and the Brooklyn Bridge, as well as books showing gorgeous but smaller bridges in Venice and Bamberg. I told myself that if I sought out books about especially lovely bridges, perhaps Zeko could be lured into becoming a bridge aficionada pure and simple, maybe even luring her into studying civil engineering. But I quickly saw that Zeko was not all that interested in these small but lovely bridges. She was always interested in their dimensions, and the bigger the better. After all, how likely was it that she would be involved in a hot pursuit over the Rialto Bridge in Venice? Not much. Get the point? Of course, Kris and I valued Zeko's valiant efforts to keep all of us safe from pollution, but Kris feared that she was enjoying her tools of trade a bit too much, especially the use of explosives. Kris had hopes for Zeko and continued to nurture dreams of her eventual rehabilitation. After all, since the stuffed rabbit knew so much about bridges, she could obviously build them just as easily, and if she could break with her "demolition habit", she wouldn't need to destroy any more bridges, right? Kris was starting to see a big future for her as a civil engineer. As for me, I could appreciate the threat posed by industrial pollution, and, as I watched the wooded habitats of Lynnwood being chopped and cleared, with massive high-rise apartments erected in their places, and as I saw the number of cars multiply, all pouring out noxious exhaust, I knew that we could use a stuffed rabbit to champion clear air. Besides, the people of Seattle had voted to slash car registration fees, and with that, the budget for public transport shriveled and even more people had no choice but to rev up their cars and take to the I-5.

Then one day, Kris and I heard on the news that the 520 bridge had sunk into Lake Washington. The news reports blamed faulty foundations. But we had our doubts. "Zeko," we called out in unison, with about the same tone of voice that a mother might adopt in berating a naughty child.

"Yes," said Zeko, doing her best to project sweet innocence.

"Did you have anything to do with this?" We pointed to the screen. Unfortunately, by then, the broadcast had switched to a commercial for a raisin cereal.

"Raisin cereal? Not my specialty," Zeko answered rather too self-righteously and started to march out.

"You know what we mean!" Kris said stiffly. "The 520 bridge. It didn't seem to have any problems until you showed up."

"Whaddyamean? Is there a problem?"

"Zeko!"

"Hey, I'm not responsible for every bridge that goes down."

"Maybe not, Zeko, but how about this one?" Kris pressed her, assuming the role of interrogator. "No casualties – that's your style, isn't it?"

"I don't know," said Zeko.

"You don't know, eh?"

"The bridge had problems."

"Come on, Zeko, fess up," I said.

"OK, Comrade, OK, Kris. I shouldn't be telling you anything at all, but let me put it this way. A downed bridge is a lot better than what would have happened otherwise. They were planning to turn the coastal front of Bellevue into an industrial site and that would have meant more pollution and more pulmonary problems for everyone. It would also have meant more people crowded into a small space, with less room for the nonhuman inhabitants of the planet. This did not look good to us. They had to be stopped!"

"Zeko, people want to drive to work."

"They can drive around the lake," Zeko pointed out.

"You know that takes twice as long," came Kris's rejoinder.

"But you have to admire the aesthetics of it. The sheer beauty of this job. I did it in such a way as to be completely undetectable. You heard for yourself that they blame it on faulty foundations, and now the city wants to sue the civil engineers who constructed the bridge! Hah!" Zeko laughed cockily. She was enjoying this moment. "Hush!"

The commercial break was over, and there was more footage of the now-sunken 520 bridge. Zeko dashed excitedly up to the television and watched it intently. Kris and I were stunned and just sat there. Only when they finished with the bridge story and turned to the next disaster did we turn off the set and attempt, once more, to confront Zeko.

But Zeko was in full stride: "Bridge destruction is an art form just like any other. Like painting or musical composition. Same thing. A good demolition has grace and form, rhythm, an external glide that corresponds to and replicates the pattern set at epicenter. It may flow like a symphony or dance like a minuet. And just as a good symphony does not produce any casualties, so too no one gets hurt when a master at bridge demolition is at work. I *love* bridges," Zeko said in conclusion, "especially when they are being artfully destroyed."

"Zeko, can't you fight pollution without destroying bridges!?" Kris asked. "Have you ever thought about flower arrangement?"

"You can't fight corporate polluters with flower arrangements!" Zeko shot back. But she was chatty and added, "We rounded them all up and took them to jail. They'll go on trial downtown. It will probably be reported on the late night news." I don't know about any laws that really restrict polluters. But maybe Zeko had in mind a People's Court.

5

A Happy Reunion

It was not long after all of this excitement that Kris decided to bring home a companion for Zeko. Since it was well past Easter by then, it was pointless to look for any remaining recruits from Zeko's unit at Bartell's. Those rabbits that had not been ransomed had been packed for storage somewhere. So Kris went to a toyshop just off Pioneer Square, bearing the unlikely name, "Magic Mouse". Here she found a large variety of stuffed rabbits to choose from. Along the top shelf were the "normals", each calling out to her, enticingly, "Buy me! Buy me!" They all had the same thing on their minds. On the second shelf were the "polemicists". They were so busy arguing with each other about "very important things" that they did not even notice the customers, unless one of their number was grabbed by a customer with a taste for constant argument. On the third row down were the "paranoids". Many of them were staring wildly, with a look of crazed fear. As Kris examined their ranks, each of them shouted, "Leave me alone! You don't want me! Buy her! Buy him! What do you want? Why me? Stop looking at me!" and so on. And finally, on the bottom row were the "apathetics". They had a dreadful view down there and mostly could see only the customers' boots. But they didn't care. Not about that. Not about anything. They were, after all, apathetic. They just stared at each other and at the customers' boots, with blank expressions on their faces. Kris didn't care for the polemicists or the paranoids or the apathetics. So she straightened up and started to pick from among the "normals". But just then her eye wandered down to the "polemicists'" shelf. At the far right sat a somewhat overweight rabbit with black and white spots, who looked very pleased with herself and totally disinterested in the polemics next door, which she was basically ignoring. Manufactured in China and graced with ears somewhat smaller than your run-of-the-mill hare, this rabbit seemed remarkably self-absorbed. In fact, this was the only rabbit in the entire store that defied the shelf-by-shelf categorization scheme. On the contrary, this unique rabbit was quite absorbed in humming an old English folk song softly to herself.

Kris bought the humming rabbit and brought her home, and, scarcely able to contain her excitement, announced to me, "I have bought a second rabbit to keep Zeko company."

"Uh-oh!" was about all the enthusiasm I could muster at that point. After all, if one stuffed rabbit could single-handedly sink the 520 bridge, what might two stuffed rabbits, acting in collaboration, be able to do? But Kris was oblivious to the risks involved and blithely placed the humming rabbit on the bed next to Zeko. She then picked up a dust rag, got down on her knees, and began to clean the rungs on our upright chairs. "There's a spot here," Kris muttered to herself. "Gotta clean it."

"Sacher!" Zeko screamed with unconcealed joy in her high-pitched voice.

"Zeko!" the now-identified Sacher squealed in a deeply resonant, and somewhat wirey, alto, with scarcely less delight.

"It's been a long time, what? Five years? Six years?"

"Something like that, Zeko! My gosh, we were a pair. Nothing could stop us."

The two rabbits in unison: "Nothing can stop us now!!"

Great, I thought to myself. Probably a fellow green anarchist-rabbit.

"So you were assigned here too, Sacher?"

"Yes, Zeko. What good fortune! Together again."

"One minute," I interrupted. "You say you were *assigned* here! Didn't we buy you off the shelves? Didn't we pick you out ourselves?"

Sacher straightened herself up and explained: "Ordinarily I wouldn't let on, but it's obvious that we can trust you. So I will tell you. We have been assigned to file reports on you two. It's standard procedure to assign two rabbits to the job."

"I thought Zeko was a rabbit eco-terrorist, not a rabbit-*spy*," I retorted, with a hint of derision.

"Oh, come," Sacher said in a low, reassuring voice, "let's not use provocative, indelicate language. And besides, our work is multifaceted, and embraces fighting the polluters, saving the planet, receptions, deceptions, mass agitation and propaganda, disinformation, manufacturing, transport, and of course these reports. We have to keep an eye on you two."

Kris was smiling broadly. I was confused. Maybe the bunnies brought back happy recollections of her old radical days. "Kris!!" I protested.

"Oh, don't worry about *them*, Bill!" Kris replied with a laugh.

"Look, I thought you were a specialist, Zeko," I objected.

"I do many things, Comrade," replied Zeko. "I, the amazing Zeko, am capable of many, many things."

"Well, I don't think I am comfortable with seeing our home converted into a center for eco-terrorist work, even if it is for a good cause!" I declared. "How are we supposed to go about our lives? And what if some corporate bosses send men in white jackets to take out our brains? Then what?"

"Perhaps you want sweet little cuddly creatures, that you could dress up in pretty dresses, eh? The kind of rabbits that would be seen and not heard," Sacher suggested. "Well, that's not us. We're very serious rabbits. We're not your gad-about, floozy sort of rabbit. We are eco-terrorists. We are committed. We have a purpose. We even have a plan. A five-year plan."

"But when you demolish things, you make a mess, don't you?" Kris asked. "And who cleans it up? You? And I imagine that you dress in rumpled clothes with silly ship captain hats, right? I mean you're eco-terrorists."

"You've been up late watching old black-and-white films," Zeko objected. "Today's eco-terrorists are very different. We all dress in up to date fashions, or at the most, in guerrilla fatigues, we do most of our secret work by day, and when we need to demolish a bridge, we first get everyone off the bridge. Then we seal off the access roads on both sides. Then we make sure that there is no one below who will get hurt. Only then do we blow up the bridge."

"And you actually catch the polluters, while taking all of these precautions?"

"You bet we do," Zeko answered.

"Your bridge demolition routine sounds really inefficient," Kris observed.

"No, it's not," Zeko replied. And then, sounding almost sanctimonious, she continued, "Waste of life is much more 'inefficient', if you want that word. Do you think we work alone? Of course not! I command a brigade of usually 40 stuffed rabbits who assist me in my work. Some of these are assigned to evacuation duty, and their sole task is to evacuate innocent by-standers..."

"OK, I get the picture. Sweet and cuddly eco-terrorists!"

"We are anarchists," explained Commander Zeko, "and as anarchists we are against the state, we are against all states."

"You are Bakuninists!" Kris gasped in horror.

"No way," said Sacher. "Bakunin was a rough sort. We work to protect human and nonhuman life, which is under threat from money-grubbing commodity-pushers whose only thought is how to get richer and how to spend their ill-gotten dollars. Like any anarchist worth his salt, we want to protect maximum liberty for everyone and to encourage people to develop community spirit."

"That makes a lot of sense," I sneered sarcastically.

"Don't be so smart, when you don't know what you are talking about."

"But all these fancy bridge demolitions cost money too, don't they?" asked Kris. "Wouldn't it be better to spend our tax dollars on supporting low-cost university education and on introducing a national healthcare plan?"

"What do you think? That we are using tax dollars to fight the polluters?" asked Sacher rhetorically. "Besides, your tax dollars are not going to help ordinary people, they are going into the pockets of the corporate rich, as so-called developmental 'incentives'. But evil must be fought. There is no turning back."

"Sacher," Zeko interjected. "Do you remember the time we were in Libya in order to learn how to disguise ourselves as camels?"

"What, did you wear fake humps?"

"Don't be so primitive. We are sophisticated eco-terrorists, remember? Masters of disguise."

"And the time," Zeko continued, "we worked with North

"Do you remember the time we were in Libya in order to learn how to disguise ourselves as camels?"

Korean experts in subliminal messages and invented punk music? Wasn't that great?"

"Oh, great days," Sacher agreed.

"Hey, wait a moment," Kris said, interrupting them. "What's this about your inventing punk music?"

"Oh you are interested, are you?" Zeko replied coyly, teasing us a little. "Sacher and I were assigned to a musical eco-terrorist squad and our assignment was to devise the most hideously ugly music imaginable, music that we could use in our operations, music that would drive people crazy, but laden with subliminal messages. The kind of music that you could play on a battlefront and drive the enemy crazy. We worked on this, in conjunction with a team of professional composers, and the result was Operation LANCE — Loud Anti-Music Noise Creation Experiment. We were sure that this was really dreadful, but then, to our complete surprise, some young people took it seriously and even claimed to like it. So we scrapped the project, though not before a couple of our comrades dropped out of the movement in order to play punk music professionally."

"That reminds me," Sacher started in, "of the time I was at a special Portuguese-language training school on the northern tip of Sakhalin --"

"On Sakhalin? For Portuguese?"

"Oh, sure. It was a very prestigious school, run by the KGB. Top secret. I was supposed to be assigned to carry out internal subversion in Portugal. But at the last minute I was given a cushy assignment and sent to infiltrate the security service in Romania and gather information on their economic planning. And I was speaking Portuguese, not Romanian. So in Transylvania, I told them I was from Bucharest, and they all knew that people in Bucharest talked a bit different. In Bucharest I told them I was from Transylvania. Sometimes with intellectuals I would tell them I was a medievalist and that I was speaking medieval Romanian. Then one day, I was introduced to Romania's leading expert on Portugal, and my explanation fell flat."

Zeko: "That reminds me of the time I was trying to make gunpowder souffle and my souffle fell flat."

"Come on, Zeko, there's no such thing as gunpowder souffle!"

Sacher: "That reminds me of the time I concocted my own alternative chocolate recipe using no cocoa at all, and the result fell flat."

Zeko: "Sacher!"

Sacher: "Zeko!"

These exclamations were exchanged with genuine warmth, as they hugged and kissed each other. And I found myself thinking back to old photos of Syrian President Hafez Assad kissing Palestinian leader Yasir Arafat, or Brezhnev kissing Erich Honecker.

"They should have told me you'd be here," Zeko said softly.

"You know as well as I do that all operations are secret," Sacher replied.

"I know, I know -- but it's so good to *see* you!"

"So have you filed any reports on these two yet?" Sacher asked earnestly.

"Not yet," Zeko replied. "I just got here. But I've been making my observations and taking notes."

"Good, good," said Sacher.

"One minute," I said. "What if we don't want you filing reports on us!"

"Yeah," Kris echoed, "I for one don't like it."

"Why does your movement, or whatever it is, need information about our private lives, anyway?" I asked.

Sacher: "Oh, that reminds me of the time I was on the French Riviera, and some visitors from California were trying to surf, but they didn't like the waves."

"That reminds me," Zeko shot back, "of the time I was assigned to round up some terrorists who were on the loose in Wabasso, but they supplied me with second-rate explosives, and I didn't like the explosives, so I did the job without using any explosives."

Sacher: "Oh, that reminds me of the time when Zeko and I were in Andorra, installing landmines in the Andorran Pyrenees. And we didn't like the local sheep, because they were bleating off-key."

"OK," I sighed, "we give up. File your reports."

"But we won't cooperate," Kris added.

6

The Truth about the Bermuda Triangle

"So who do you work for anyway?" Kris asked the rabbits, as if they hadn't been boasting about it all along.

"We're green anarchists, remember? And anarchists," Sacher replied, with a touch of pride.

"But someone is paying your salary, surely. Probably one or another government. And you can't be an anarchist if you want to work for the government," said Kris, who fancied tidy explanations.

The rabbits seemed offended at this suggestion, and Zeko immediately objected, "No, we have our principles. We would only work for a government which would interested in promoting anarchist principles, a government working toward its own self-dissolution."

"And we wage a relentless struggle against the proliferation of diesel smoke, which, as you know, exemplifies *particulate matter*. How big are these particles?" Sacher asked. We all held our breath hoping that she would not answer her own question. But she did: "These particles typically measure about 2.5 microns or about .0001 inches across and are also called 'black carbon' pollution. Have you ever considered the exhaust from your car or from the nearby factory? Well, these are bad things and we blow up pollutant factories in the interest of life and good times."

"That's right," Zeko said, "and we protect the environment at the same time. We are eco-eco-terrorists (twice as ecological as your run-of-the-mill eco-terrorists), defending the planet from the self-destructive machinations of industrial polluters. We fight capitalism in an environmentally friendly way, we use our explosives with close attention to the effects of our explosives on the environment, and we help the exploiters to repent and mend their ways. We destroy the weapons of fascists, militant terrorists, and honey-terrorists, who try to hide weapons and drugs in the honey, and other right-wingers, and help them to give up their destructive ways and to convert to a life of tolerance and gentleness."

"Education is a major component of our work as eco-terrorists," Sacher said, grinning broadly.

"Education is a central component of any eco-terrorism worthy of the name," said Zeko, seconding Sacher. "Eco-terrorists who do not educate are charlatans, not the real thing."

"OK, we're impressed," I replied.

"Who do *you* work for?" came Sacher's reply.

"Oh, that's a silly question," Kris and I said.

"So if it's so silly, don't pose that silly question to us!" Zeko commanded.

"OK," Kris said, in a tone that implied a concession. "But I have another question. You two are girl-rabbits, right?"

"Of course!"

"So why don't you have more explicitly female names," Kris asked, forgetting that her own name was not exactly a classic example of an explicitly female name. "I mean, people want to know the sex of persons they are about to meet, or really anyone at all."

"Yes," I agreed, "that's what people always want to know first -- what's the person's sex."

"Well, I for one don't know why a person's sex should be so interesting. I think it's much more useful to know a person's *species*," Sacher mused, "especially when you consider that the different species have very different talents and abilities. Of course, if you are meeting a person face-to-face, you usually don't have to check the name to figure out what species the person is. It's usually pretty obvious. And this is much more useful information than knowing a person's sex. For example, if someone is a tiger, maybe you want to think twice before inviting it -- whether him or her -- to your birthday party. Of course, most species have their good points."

Zeko interjected: "Jellyfish are *boring!* If they say anything at all, it is only the most banal drib-drab. Things on the order of, 'The water is wet,' 'It is getting cold now,' or 'I want to sting someone.' Nothing more profound than that. Someone threw a surprise birthday party for me once and invited a lot of jellyfish. Boy, was that ever a boring party! And you had to be careful about shaking hands too!"

"But on the whole," Sacher observed, "rabbits make the best company."

"Rabbits should rule the world, you know," Zeko pointed out. "Rabbit rule is best."

"Just a minute," I objected, remembering some of the things I had learned in political science classes, "how would rabbits rule? How would you set up a bureaucracy?"

"If rabbits ruled the world," Zeko replied, "there would be more carrot fields and more lettuce patches, and it would be illegal to sell rabbit-foot charms." Zeko and Sacher broke into cheesy grins, looking very pleased with themselves.

"So you really don't care what sex a person is, then."

"I'd be more interested in knowing if someone has been to Libya," Zeko replied.

"Why, on earth?"

"Because it's interesting!"

"That's not interesting."

"It is to us," Sacher replied. "It could be significant."

"Well, knowing a person's sex is interesting to us."

"That's right," Sacher recalled. "When humans have a baby, the first thing other humans want to know is what its sex is."

"OK," I challenged, "what do *you* think is the most important thing to know about a baby? -- whether it's been to Libya yet?"

"Oh, you're making fun, again," Sacher said with an air of joviality. "Assuming that you already know its species, I think it would be interesting to know if good dancing genes run in the family."

Zeko had something to say: "And whether the hands show promise of becoming muscular, and whether the fingers look like they'll be nimble, so that they can handle heavy loads of dynamite. That's what I want to know when someone has a baby."

"OK, Zeko. I see your point. But we humans, in our simple ways, are unable to think ahead to a baby's possible future career as an eco-terrorist. So we wonder about its sex, and maybe, if you're lucky, how much the child weighs and whether it's healthy."

"How much the child weighs!" Zeko seemed outraged. "Who should care? What do you want to do? -- sell it by the pound?"

"No Zeko, it's just..., it's just interesting."

"To you maybe," Zeko replied. "It's not interesting to me. I'd be more interested in the nimbleness of the fingers."

That afternoon the rabbits were hard at work at their desk, on which they seemed to have a large map spread out. Kris was curious and, pretending to clean the windows, she maneuvered herself to the vicinity of the rabbits' map. There were various books piled up next to the map, with titles such as *Project Bluebook, Project Silverbird, The Roswell Incident, Area 51 Revisited,* and *The Life and Times of Kenneth Arnold.*

"Top secret, top secret," the rabbits chanted, rolling up the map as Kris approached, and covering up the books.

"Oh, come on, guys," Kris said, trying to be her sweetest. "We don't object if you file reports on us. We'll even help you. But we're interested in your work."

"Go away, go away, top secret," Zeko said, in a nervous voice. "It's none of your business."

"That's right," Sacher added. "If you needed to know about the Bermuda Triangle, we would share our information. But this is on a need-to-know basis, strictly."

"You didn't have to tell her all that," Zeko fumed at Sacher. "Just tell her it's secret."

But, of course, the cat was out of the bag, at least partly. "The Bermuda Triangle," I said, beaming. I was getting very excited. "That's always been a special interest of Kris's. Right Kris?"

"If you say so," she replied.

"So why are you two interested in the Bermuda Triangle?" I asked.

"OK," Sacher said. "I'll tell you everything -- "

Zeko: "No, Sacher, don't do it!"

Sacher: "The Bermuda Triangle is actually a trapezoid. It should be called the Bermuda Trapezoid. This is why there have been so many mysteries surrounding it. And we want to identify its mid-point."

Zeko: "Yes, that's it. That's it. Now, go away. We're busy."

Kris: "Why do you want to locate the mid-point?"

Zeko: "Because it's interesting. Interesting to us. Now, go away. Go away. Top secret, top secret."

Kris tells me that the rabbits never talk when I'm not around. And I have seen for myself that they never talk when she is not around. I don't know what that means. But I do know that much of the time they seem to be talking primarily to her, not to me... So when Kris left the house to go browsing for mysteries, the rabbits immediately went to sleep, and, for the life of me, they looked completely inanimate. If I hadn't known better, I might have thought that they were just dolls or something.

But late that evening, after Kris had returned, she sat down in the "comfortable" chair and began to write a letter to our friend, Kazuko. Kris didn't notice as the rabbits took up positions on either side of her and began to read her letter, over her shoulders as it were or, more truthfully, over her elbows. Evidently she was telling Kazuko about the rabbits, because Zeko and Sacher now became very agitated.

"What's this?" Zeko asked. "A *report! You* are filing reports on *us!*"

"Well, well, the truth comes out," Sacher said with a smirk. "So who do *you* work for?"

7

Where's your tag?

It was about a month after the rabbits' reunion. I was sitting in the living room listening to Jasha Horenstein's stirring performance of Sibelius' Symphony No. 5, with the BBC Symphony Orchestra, when Kris came bounding through the door, with an air of wild excitement. At first I thought it was the music that had stirred her, but she quickly disabused me of any such illusions.

"Bill," she nearly shouted. "The Arc of Splendour has been blown up."

"What?!" I said.

"The Arc of Splendour Fine Treats candy store! Somebody blew it up!"

"Too bad they didn't hit the Brain Surgery Clinic too," I mused.

"But they *did!* They shattered several windows, and threw

smoke bombs into the clinic. But that's only the beginning. They also blew up Green Lake Machine Parts, Finster Chemicals, and the Hydropak Tire Company."

"*Who* did? You don't say who!"

"They don't know yet, but whoever did it, they also completely leveled the Arc of Splendour Glue Factory."

"It was the work of eco-terrorists, but we managed to rescue those animals that were still alive," Zeko pointed out.

"Now you're sure that you two weren't behind this, being anarchists and all," Kris challenged.

"Hey, don't be so rough on them, Kris," I interjected. "After all, whoever did this hit the brain surgeons too."

"You're not content with having a nice comfortable home with all the plastic carrots you could possibly want," Kris went on. "You're not content to have Astrolabe and Sextant to play with. No, you have to run around destroying other people's property."

"Untrue," Sacher said in a strong rebound. "It is the polluters and brain surgeons and land developers who are destroying other people's lives and property, even their brains. It is the exploiters who are destroying the common property we all share -- rabbits, peacocks, cats, humans alike. There is no right to destroy the eco-system. We did *not* blow up these facilities, but Seattle is probably better off without these particular facilities. Why should Green Lake be turned into a putrescent toxic cesspool for industrial waste? Why should Seattle's children be encouraged to live on a diet of toxic sulfo-candies?"

"Are you going to capture the terrorists?" Kris wondered out loud.

"Our operations are clandestine," Zeko pointed out, "and we make sure that nobody gets hurt. We only level with you because we trust you. But apparently the operations were completely clean: no clues, no mistakes, no casualties, and above all, no calling card. But it wasn't us."

"Face it, Kris," I said, "they just might know what they are talking about."

"And I thought that they were just eco-anarchists," Kris moaned. "But it turns out that they are eco-eco-terrorists!"

They don't pay rent, but they don't eat much either. In fact, they don't eat anything at all, as far as I can tell, being *stuffed* rabbits, although they talk interminably about carrots and lettuce and pomegranates. Who has ever heard of a rabbit eating pomegranates? Or, for that matter, who has ever heard of a *stuffed* rabbit eating *anything*? But the rabbits say they earn their keep. They say that they protect us.

They call us their "humans", as if we were their pets or something. OK, maybe we are, at least in their eyes. The world looks a little different if you're a rabbit, as Zeko has repeatedly pointed out. Zeko is always pointing out valuable lessons to us.

But thank goodness for Sacher! She has had a real calming effect on Zeko, at least to some extent. Zeko flies off the handle so easily. Given half a chance, I think she would blow up every bridge within a 100-mile radius, even if one or another bridge had no connection with the fight against pollution. Sacher helps Zeko to keep her focus on the fact that their acts of bridge demolition must serve to promote the survival of the planet, the survival of species, and good times.

But Sacher sometimes lets Zeko push her around, or talk her into unnecessary things. For example, one day the four of us were sitting around reading. The rabbits were decoding a secret transmission from an unknown source, when Sacher suddenly told us, "Zeko gave me my shot today."

"What shot?" Kris and I asked.

"My shot. Zeko said I needed a shot."

"But you're not ill, Sacher. You don't need any shots!" Zeko seemed to have disappeared momentarily.

"She even volunteered to give it to me."

"I'll bet she did. And where, pray tell, do you get this shot?"

"In the butt."

"Of course, I should have guessed," and then, turning, with my best authoritative air, to our other rabbit, I said, "Zeko, Zeko, wherever you are!" Zeko emerged from behind the cushion. "What's the meaning of this?"

"You stay out of this!" Zeko ordered.

"Zeko knows best," said Sacher with her usual calm certainty.

Our protests were quite unavailing. Zeko had prescribed injections in the butt, and Sacher seemed quite convinced that if Zeko said she needed them, then she needed them.

We soon got used to it. About every two weeks, they would reenact the same ritual. Zeko would squeal with unconcealed excitement, "Time for your shot, Sacher!" often with stress on the word "shot". Sacher would then brace herself against the headboard and expose her butt to full view. Zeko proved to be the quintessential expert. She had an enormous supply of syringes evidently, and removing each as necessary, she expertly tightened the needle and then confidently plunged it into a bottle containing some unknown substance, drawing it up. As she did all this, her eyes danced playfully.

Once the syringe was ready, Zeko took out a cottonball, poured some rubbing alcohol onto it, and wiped off a small section of Sacher's butt. She then picked up the syringe, went to the far end of the bed, and began to run toward Sacher. Halfway across the bed, she took a flying leap at Sacher, holding the syringe in front of her like a lance. As she plunged the syringe into Sacher's butt, Sacher would always groan loudly. It was a groan that seemed to mix both pain and pleasure.

It was in the course of one of these "medical interventions", that Zeko suddenly noticed a rather prominent tag sticking out from the middle of Sacher's back. She read it with interest:

"All new materials
Stuffing: 100% polyester fiber
Machine wash, cool (in pillowcase)
mild detergent.
Tumble dry, low (in pillowcase).
Made in China.
This label is affixed in compliance
with The Upholstered and Stuffed
Articles Act.
This article contains new material only."

"Made in China! I always thought you were Libyan or Italian," Zeko exclaimed. "So how come you don't speak any Chinese?"

"I left China at a young age, for my first assignment," Sacher explained. "That training in Libya. So I always felt more connection with Libya than with China."

"And all new materials," Kris commented, straightening a vase. "Sounds good."

Sacher examined Zeko's back, touching her gently with what was as much a caress as a probe. "Where's your tag? It's not on your back!"

"I don't know," Zeko replied. "It's somewhere."

"Let me see," Sacher urged.

"Yes, come on, Zeko," Kris offered her own encouragement.

"Leave me alone, it's my tag!" Zeko protested.

"Oh, come on, Zeko, comrade," Sacher emphasized this last word. "We work together and play together. The least you can do is show me your tag."

"OK, Sacher, for the sake of comradeship," Zeko said, sounding like a chastened revolutionary.

So Zeko gave up her resistance, and the three of us found her tag: "Zeko," I said to her, "your tag is in your butt!" We all giggled with amusement, all of us except, of course, Zeko.

"I don't see what's so funny," came Zeko's retort. "I *like* it there."

Sacher bent down and read Zeko's tag to us:

"10-inch Feather rabbit.
Eco-terrorist model.
All new materials
Stuffed with Polyester Fiber
Mild detergent, tumble dry
This label is affixed in compliance
with the Upholtered and Stuffed Articles Act.
Made in Thailand."

"See," Zeko said with gratification, "I'm also made with all new materials."

"And you're both stuffed with polyester fiber. Definitely a pair."

"OK, Comrade, where's *your* tag? Kris, where's *your* tag? Fair's fair. We showed you our tags. Now you show us yours," Zeko said.

"Zeko, we don't *have* tags," Kris replied.

"Everyone has a tag," said Sacher, very confidently. "I saw it at the factory. No stuffed animal leaves the factory without a tag. Tags are required under the provisions of the Upholstered and Stuffed Articles Act."

"But Sacher," I tried to explain, "we're not stuffed. We're humans. Our bodies are 80% water. No polyester fiber."

"No polyester!"

"Not stuffed!"

"They sent us to file reports on two non-stuffed humans," Sacher said to Zeko, with evident surprise.

"What do you need with so much water in your bodies anyway?" Zeko asked, as if objecting to the whole concept.

"It's a law of biology," Kris answered.

"So if you're not stuffed, how can you talk?" Sacher asked us.

"I don't believe it, Sacher. They're holding out on us. They have tags somewhere," Zeko said.

"What can we do to prove to you that we're telling you the truth?" I asked.

"You could start by showing us your tags," Sacher suggested.

"Wait, I have an idea," Kris said, with an inspired air. "X-rays. We'll have X-rays taken of all of us, and then the rabbits can see what we look like inside."

"So, do you think these X-rays will be covered by our medical insurance?" I asked.

8

Off to Sapporo

"**Y**ou want a *what?!*" exclaimed Mr. Mild, the X-ray technician.

"A family portrait, a full-body X-ray of us and our rabbits."

"Of these two stuffed animals?" Mr. Mild asked incredulously. "I think you need some other department. Not the X-ray department."

"No," Kris explained, smiling firmly, "we want to see what's inside."

"We understand that medical insurance probably won't cover the cost of X-raying the rabbits -- " I began.

"*Probably!?!*" Mr. Mild started. "It *definitely* won't cover it, and how can I justify even *individual* shots of you two to the insurance company, let alone some sort of 'family portrait', as you call it. Medical insurance doesn't ordinarily pay to satisfy people's curiosity." I was starting to wonder if he deserved his name.

"We will happily pay for all the X-rays, please," said Kris sweetly. "It would mean a lot to us."

"Please," I added.

The rabbits were completely still. They gave every appearance of being regular stuffed animals, nothing more.

"I could lose my license if the medical board ever found out about it," Mr. Mild said, but his tone of voice told us he was already giving in. There was a moment's pause, and then he said, "OK, come back at 5:30, after closing, and I'll take them then, but only from the neck down."

We considered going to a diner and getting a coffee, but when the rabbits started to hint that they would want to inspect the menu to see if the restaurant was serving up dead animals for people to eat, we decided that it might be best just to stay put. So we waited in his lobby. After all, it was only a four-hour wait. The rabbits, of course, had their own chairs. Some people stared at them and us, and I couldn't help wondering was this the first time they had ever seen stuffed rabbits. We had some tea while we waited. The rabbits, of course, didn't want any. After the little discussion about the restaurant, they were on their best behavior, looking as stuffed as we could have hoped for. So there were no further embarrassing and unforeseen developments.

Finally, at 5:32 p.m., the last patients left, the outer door was locked, and Mr. Mild called for us to come in. There was a small difficulty at first because we still had in mind a "family portrait".

"Look," he said, "this whole thing is wacky, but I'm willing to play along, and I'm not even going to ask you why you want an X-ray of your stuffed rabbits. But you will have to accept that I do not do 'family portraits'. I do 'individual portraits' only. Take it or leave it."

"Can you touch it up a little to make me look younger?" Zeko asked Mr. Mild, but he didn't seem to hear her.

"OK, Miss," Mr. Mild signalled to Kris. He took Kris's 'portrait' first, and then mine. Then it was Zeko's turn. But of course Zeko refused to walk and we had to carry her: talk about a regal life! That's when the trouble began.

"Oooh, that tickles," Zeko declared as Mr. Mild turned the X-ray machine on. Zeko then started giggling uncontrollably. Sacher joined in, and pretty soon, Kris and I were laughing too.

"What is this, some sort of prank?" Mr. Mild asked. "I'm willing to do this, but if you're going to laugh, I'll throw you out."

"We're really sorry," I apologized. "But when Zeko started to giggle -- "

"Oh, I get it," Mr. Mild said, suddenly sounding extra-gentle. "The X-ray tickled your little bunny, and she started laughing. OK, fine. Now let's X-ray your other little bunny."

"We're not 'little bunnies,'" Sacher objected, betraying some hurt feelings. "We're rabbits."

"Sshhh!" Kris signalled to Sacher.

"Yes, bunny," said Mr. Mild to Sacher in a kindly tone of voice, "just be still and everything will be fine."

"We're not bunnies, we're rabbits!"

"They're not bunnies, they're rabbits," I explained, in case Mr. Mild could not hear Sacher.

"Well, we don't want to offend our rabbit customers, do we?" Mr. Mild said in that same kindly tone, which was starting to sound grating. He hit the switch, the machine hummed, and *voilà*, the last X-ray was taken.

Moments later, Mr. Mild spread the four X-rays on his illuminated panel for us to see. "You two look healthy, normal bones and muscles, everything normal," Mr. Mild told us.

"We didn't X-ray your heads so we can't say anything about that." He chuckled.

"What's he chuckling about?" Sacher asked. "Is it a joke?"

"The rabbits are also normal," Mr. Mild assured us, adding, "for stuffed toys. No bones, no muscles, just polyester fiber."

"All new materials!" Zeko shouted boastfully.

"See, rabbits, what did we tell you?" I said in a satisfied tone.

"Oh, did I help to settle an argument?" Mr. Mild asked. "Well good. I'll send you the bill. Now please, take these pictures with you. And please, if you ever need any more 'portraits' from me, please check with the psychiatrist's office first."

"Thank you," we said, looking at each other. No fear, we didn't plan to return to *him*. We don't need a family photographer who makes wisecracks and won't even include our heads in the photos. Or take a 'family portrait'. Obviously a screwball.

The rabbits seem, all too often, to set the agenda in our household. It was therefore quite consistent with this arrangement that we found ourselves, one afternoon, sitting in the living room, listening to a "sound effects" record that the rabbits had procured somewhere. I must say that this was the first time I had ever heard "sound effects" tracks of the sound of carrots growing, or of insects falling off lettuce leaves, or of rabbits eating carrots. These sounds did nothing for me, and frankly, I'd much rather listen to Arturo Toscanini conducting Tchaikovsky's Symphony No. 5 any day, but the rabbits seemed utterly enthralled, almost in a trance. I was therefore a bit surprised when Sacher suddenly pointed out, "The mail has arrived."

"So are you waiting for something?" I asked.

"We're always waiting for something," Zeko countered. "We have contacts and collaborators all over the world."

"I don't think I want to know about them," I said, as I went out to bring in the mail. I returned bouncing off the walls with exultation.

"This doesn't look good," said Zeko to Sacher. "News this good usually means trouble."

"Easy, Zeko," Sacher said, trying to reassure her. "Maybe it won't be a complete catastrophe."

"So what is it? What is it?" Kris asked.

"We're going to Sapporo!" I announced jubilantly. "My project has been approved. We'll be in Japan for 10 glorious months."

"Great!" said Kris.

"Japan? Ten months? Why weren't we consulted about this?" Zeko began. "Our work is here in Seattle."

"Hey rabbits, you can still file reports on us in Japan," I tried to reassure them.

"Oh you think you're the be-all and end-all of our lives, do you?" Zeko shot back. "Our surveillance of you two is only one facet of our work. But this will affect all of our work. We have set up our base of operations here. All of our eco-terrorist work is centered on Seattle. Oh, this is dreadful, just dreadful..."

"Hold on, Zeko," said Sacher. "Let's look on the bright side. We can expand our eco-terrorist operations to Japan, and, for that matter, there's an important sewage museum in Nagoya which we can visit; it might give us some additional ideas for the next time we want to demolish a sewage system. In Tokyo we can examine the Shibaura sewage disposal facility, which offers guided tours, and also the Koto Incineration Plant, which even sells postcards."

"Postcards? You're making this up," Kris objected.

"Have you been there?"

"No."

"Well then, you should take notes."

"And then there's the Sunamachi sewage disposal facility too," Zeko said with rising excitement.

"And not only that. We can also examine the materials held at the Tokyo Archives for Combatting Terrorism," Sacher pointed out. "After all, we need to keep up with the latest techniques of our enemies."

"And maybe we can look up some of our old war buddies," Zeko said, beaming broadly, adding, for our benefit, "We were together in the Bekaa Valley."

"And best of all, we can look up our good friend, il Dottore Ottavio del Paese," Sacher pointed out.

"OK, we'll go!" Zeko announced.

"Please arrange for a special carrot and lettuce lunch service for us," Sacher suggested.

"And we don't want to depart any earlier than noon, so we can sleep in."

"And don't forget, we always fly first-class," said Sacher.

"You won't be flying first-class this time unless you pay for your own seats."

"Not riding first class! This is humiliating," Zeko said in a loud voice. "I hate riding in coach. There's not enough leg room."

"Oh, don't worry, Zeko," I said in a reassuring tone of voice, "you won't be riding in coach either. You'll be in the baggage."

"In the baggage!!" the rabbits shrieked in unison.

"This is an absolute outrage!"

"I'll report you to the Society for the Prevention of Cruelty to Stuffed Animals!"

"Zeko, Sacher," said Kris. "We can't afford to buy tickets for you guys. If you want to fly in the coach with us or even in first class, perhaps you can buy your own tickets. After all, don't you have a pretty ample fund for your work? I mean, Green Anarchy ought to pay for your tickets."

"Our operations fund is all tied up in gold bars right now," Sacher explained. "And it's hard to sell off gold bars on short notice." She did not explain why they had so much money or why it was all in gold bars. But I was starting to get the feeling that we already knew too much about their work.

For a couple of famous eco-terrorists, they didn't put up much of a fight. We stuffed them into our suitcases, along with our clothes, our year's supply of Q-tips, my binoculars, my roller skates, Kris's leather pants and skirts, and Kris's copies of the Greater Chronicles of the Venerable Bede and of the meditations of Julian of Norwich. They were grumbling the whole way to the airport. They kept returning to this theme that this was a great cruelty, a great injustice. Astrolabe and Sextant were much more cooperative. We took the precaution of giving them a muscle relaxant, and this left them in a torpid state. We didn't dare even suggest to the rabbits that they take muscle relaxants. We had enough trouble on our hands without going out of our way to provoke it.

Checking in the luggage proved to be a major hurdle. The cats were quiet enough. But the rabbits just kept it up: "Help, let us out of here, we're prisoners! Help, let us out! This is an outrage!" And they started kicking and rolling around, so that the suitcase in which we had put them started to rock back and forth.

"Good morning and thank you for flying with Enchanted Airlines," said the airline functionary with the plastic smile on his lips. "Will that be smoking or non-smoking? Aisle or window? Did you pack your own bags? Did anyone ask you to carry anything on board? Have you kept your eyes glued on your luggage at all times? Are you carrying any sharp objects? Are you members of the Enchanted Mileage Club? No, well I can register you if you would like to travel to enchanted places free of charge. And how many pieces of luggage? Eleven?"

"*None* until we're out of here!" Zeko screamed, as the two rabbits lunged against the side of the suitcase. The suitcase nearly toppled over.

"Just ignore that," Kris said, straightening the credit card application box and luggage tags on the counter. "Eleven is correct."

"Ignore that? Yes, right. Eleven it is." The airline functionary had a slightly odd look about him suddenly. "Let's take this heavy one first, shall we?"

"No you don't," Sacher advised. "This isn't any way for a self-respecting airline to behave. What is this, a penal colony airline?"

"We don't necessarily agree with everything our luggage says," I said at this point. It seemed best to stay on the safe side.

"With your luggage?" the functionary replied. "Hello? -- Hey Susan! I've got a live one here."

"I guess he couldn't hear them after all," I muttered to Kris.

"Let us out or we'll blow up the plane in mid-flight!" Zeko screamed at the top of her lungs. I bit my tongue. Kris put on an air of dumb innocence. And somehow we got checked in, they took the baggage, all of it. We got our boarding passes. And the last we saw of the rabbits' suitcase before reaching Japan, it was rocking back and forth as the conveyor belt carried them off to be loaded onto the plane.

Kris and I breathed a huge sigh of relief and went to the coffee house, carrying our caged felines, to spend our last hour before departure in peace and quiet. Kris wanted to enjoy her last café latte for 10 months, in spite of my frenzied warnings about prozac and other drugs in the coffee. But I will confess that there is usually something quite pleasant about seeing so many drugged people in the same place, all with the same vapid expressions of felicity bordering on stupor on their faces. The entire coffee house smelled of marzipan, or at least I hoped it was marzipan. It also might have been some sort of cleaner, you know, one of those super cleaners that can remove *any* bad scent, like what they use in hospitals. The coffee house had the usual pleasant look about it -- at first sight -- except for the television, perched up near the ceiling so that the customers could watch the outcome of the latest sporting events. But just as I was about to decide on what kind of macaroon to order, a commercial started up on the TV. A deep, authoritative male voice intoned:

"Does your brain ache? Do you suffer from brain decay? Well, if you answered yes to these questions, we have good news for you. Our trained mentists can help. We use the latest technology, including brain scans, brain drills, and brain fillings. We can remove the decay painlessly, and even brush and floss your brain. Remember: regular brain check-ups, brushings, and no thinking between meals -- and you can have a healthier, stronger brain. And on your first visit, we'll even throw in a special gift of whitener that you can use right in your own home."

I looked around the coffee house and it was only now that I noticed that all of the other customers had their heads bandaged, like they had just had brain surgery or something. Only the barista, the fellow in the blue gown, didn't have his head bandaged.

"Kris," I said with rising alarm, "we've got to get out of here." I got up and started for the exit.

"What's wrong?" said Kris, as she followed after me. "Oh, I guess you don't want to watch sports." Perhaps she didn't notice all the customers with their heads bandaged up. Doesn't have a trained eye like mine. Never miss a detail.

... it was only now that I noticed that all of the other customers had their heads bandaged.

The image of that coffee house, filled with brain surgery patients, haunted me all the way to Sapporo. I couldn't stop thinking about it, even as I was choking half to death on tobacco smoke in the middle of the unenforced "no smoking" area. It's a plot, I kept repeating to myself, in an effort to reassure myself that there was some "logical" explanation.

9

Opening
Café Bombshell

I will admit that I had been a little worried about Japanese security. After all, we were only bringing two green anarchists in our baggage. But Kris and I banked on the Japanese officials being fooled by their appearance. We had to open our suitcases, and the official actually picked up the rabbits, and, chuckling, said to us, "What are these? A couple of green anarchists?" He chuckled some more, put the rabbits back, and waved us through. I hate people with semi-intuitive senses of humor. They make my stomach turn.

It was soon after we had unpacked and settled in that we noticed that Zeko was unusually quiet, and seemed to have lapsed into deep depression. Sacher seemed very concerned, and was holding her close, trying to cheer her up. Zeko remained like this for two days, not saying a word.

Then the dam broke and Zeko let everyone know what was going on. Zeko, it turned out, was having some sort of nervous breakdown and was talking about giving up her work as an eco-terrorist and becoming a fashion model. She spent her time parading around the way fashion models do, pretending to be showing off the newest elegant attire from Milano. Sacher was just down in the dumps about this, and didn't seem to know what to do.

"You can't be a fashion model," Sacher pleaded with Zeko. "You can't throw away all those years of training, all that expertise, all your contacts. Zeko, you're a professional! You have duties, and skills. Don't waste your talents!"

"You can't do this to me," Sacher implored Zeko. "Think of all the times we spent together, training at Fort Bragg, not to mention with the North Koreans in Libya. Zeko, don't do this to me!"

"You can't throw in the towel, Zeko." Sacher tried again and again. "Think of your responsibilities to the cause. Think of all the comrades who depend on you, who look to you with respect and awe, who consider you a dedicated comrade and, some say, the more fearsome eco-terrorist of all time."

"I want to be a fashion model," Zeko said to this, and every other effort on Sacher's part.

Then it was Sacher's turn to be quiet. But Sacher was thinking, and thinking hard. Sacher was not about to abandon her comrade, but she wasn't keen on this 'fashion model' concept. Some two weeks passed before Sacher finally hit on an idea. Sacher looked like she'd been struck by lightning. "We'll open a café!" she announced.

I fully expected Zeko to reject this out of hand and to insist on going into fashions. But instead, they started to negotiate, to compromise, to brainstorm. From Sacher's point of view, a café afforded the prospect of a convincing front, behind which they could continue their operations, while, from Zeko's point of view, a café might afford a welcome respite from the relentless struggle for social justice. They started talking about the name. Zeko wanted the name to convey some implication of fashions and fashion models. Sacher wanted the name to have clear associations with the fight against terror. They seemed deadlocked. This was becoming a concern for the whole family.

Zeko suggested calling it Café Mode. Sacher countered with The Bullet Café. Zeko rejected this and proposed to call the place The High Heel. Sacher rejected this and suggested instead Café Dynamite. I suggested that what they needed was to compromise, and suggested a rather transparent option: Café Compromise. They both hated that idea. Finally, Kris came up with a suggestion, "Why not call it Café Bombshell?" Zeko's eyes lit up with satisfaction. Sacher smiled warmly. We had crossed that hurdle.

After that, things moved quickly. They bought some property and hired their staff, luring one of Sapporo's best chefs to give up his job of 18 years at Ambrosia French Restaurant in order to take charge of their kitchen. They also came up with a motto for the place, which they emblazoned on a large sign affixed on the roof: "Café Bombshell—Where Eco-terrorists and Cultural Subversives Meet."

Café Bombshell opened amid controversy. First there was the "opening day" parade. They somehow arranged to "rent" some of the animals in the zoo—about 120 of them in all, and then marched them through the town, down the Odori and through the main shopping district, past Sapporo Station and Keio Plaza Hotel, and through the Botanical Garden. They hired a band to play the "Babes in Toyland" march and other march hits, and here they were—elephants, rhinos, black bears, polar bears, giraffes, platypusses, hip-pocketed kangaroos, right-handed hyenas, zebras with reversed stripes, pool sharks, paper tigers, dark horses, fat cats, pack rats, grease monkeys, lounge lizards, spring chickens, left-wing gorillas, jail birds, stool pigeons, eager beavers, and book worms, not to mention the insect participants: social butterflies, litter bugs, and shutter-bugs -- all strutting through town to advertise Café Bombshell. This spectacle quickly produced protests from local animal rights activists.

Bringing up the rear of the parade was a troupe of lathe operators, who were even singing a song about their profession. Since I always carry a notepad and pen with me, I quickly wrote down the words. Although I had to write quickly, I think their song went like this:

I wake up in the mornin' an' get out of bed
I feel so sleepy that I feel half dead
I brush ma teeth an' I scrub ma head
Gotta get ma coffee an' a piece of bread.
I jump in the tub an' start my bathin'
But I can't wait to do some lathin'.
Cause I'm a lathe operator
A lathe operator
When I turn on my lathe, I'm on top of the world
Cause I'm a lathe operator,
I'm a lathe operator an' I just can't get enough.

I work ma shift an' I'm done at five
Then I get in ma car an' I start to drive
Tomorrow I'll be back for another eight,
I wanna get up early so I won't be late.
Cause whatever I do I'm always cravin'
To get back to work and do some lathin'
Cause I'm a lathe operator
A lathe operator
When I turn on my lathe, I'm on top of the world
Cause I'm a lathe operator,
I'm a lathe operator an' I just can't get enough.

There was even a brief scuffle in the middle of the parade. A German tourist was taking photos furiously, or at least one must hope it was a tourist; it might, after all, have been a spy posing as a tourist. He kept muttering "schoen" to himself, or "wirklich schoen," and then took another photo. He was just taking a photo of the high-strutting flamingoes, when I saw a group of men in blue gowns, their hair hidden under their scrubs, rush out, grab the "tourist", place him on a gurney, strap him down, and haul him away. "Kris, did you see that?" I pressed her. But she had been looking the other way, completely oblivious to the mischief being perpetrated right under her nose. I couldn't help thinking back to the coffee house at SeaTac Airport. Brain surgeons. Here they were again. For the time being, however, I kept my deepening concerns to myself.

Meantime, the rabbits also had to deal with a certain amount of fuss about the admission fee. It might have been a lot simpler if they had just agreed on a 5,000-yen admission fee and left it at that. But being the musical rabbits they are, they decided to offer a discount rate to any customers (regardless of species) who would croon a romantic ballad for them. Crooners were admitted for only 1,000 yen. This rather substantial discount inspired a great deal of crooning, and locals were soon treated to the crooning of orangutans, cats, dogs, goats, humans, hippos, and yes, rabbits too. Some said that waiting in line was as entertaining as the shows inside.

Then there was the furor over the baseball game which they decided to stage to drum up publicity for their club: Bulgarian Bicycle Baseball with Bugles, as they called it. The game, as they explained it, was played the same as regular baseball, except that all players had to be riding bicycles for all plays. That meant pitcher, catcher, basemen, outfielders, and batters were all on bicycles for the play. Assuming the batter could somehow hit the ball while balancing on the bicycle, he was then obliged to *cycle* to first base. While cycling, he was required to blow on a bugle hanging by a strap around his neck. That was, as I understood it, the essence of Bulgarian

Bicycle Baseball with Bugles. The few fans who turned out for this spectacle were mostly confused by what was going on, and seem to have had in mind an entirely different, more traditional concept of baseball.

But gradually things settled down, and life became more "normal", whatever that means. But about two months after the Club's opening, Zeko started to complain: "Why aren't there any festivals to celebrate rabbits?"

"That's right," said Sacher. "Like a National Celebration of Rabbits on July 14."

"That's Bastille Day," I pointed out.

"So it's already taken, is it?" Sacher mused.

"And why aren't there more Fridays in a week?" Zeko asked. "Everyone likes Friday. If we just had a few more Fridays, everyone would be happy. Let's circulate a petition to rename Wednesday and Thursday so we can have three Fridays in a row!"

"Why do people underestimate the comfort and efficiency of travel by submarine?"

"Why don't they teach classes on bomb safety in the elementary schools? Don't they know that safety is important?"

"Why don't they require Senators to speak in rhymed couplets during sessions of the Senate?"

"Why don't motorboats have a reverse gear?"

"Why is there no Chamber of Rabbits in the legislature? Why are there no rabbits represented in *any* government you can find? Why are the interests of rabbits totally ignored?"

"Why don't they pick up the garbage three times a day instead of just once a week?"

"Oh come on, rabbits! You don't produce that much garbage! *We* don't!"

The rabbits glared at me for a moment. But then, as if distracted to distraction, Sacher resumed the litany: "Why don't they have showers on passenger airlines?"

Zeko quickly replied, "Why do we never hear about ghosts haunting shipwrecks at the bottom of the sea?"

"And why don't space aliens have pets?"

"And why doesn't *Time* magazine devote an issue to the Rabbit of the Year?"

"Then we could see your picture on the cover, Zeko," said Sacher with sincere and genuine enthusiasm. "That would be wonderful!"

"Why don't they let the canoers face each other in the canoe?"

"It's because -- "

"These are complaints. These are not questions at all," I pointed out.

" OF COURSE THESE AREN'T QUESTIONS! THEY'RE REFLECTIONS! They're reflections, you might say," Sacher explained.

"They're gripes!"

"We're not griping! And besides, what's wrong with griping? And besides, why doesn't the Bill of Rights protect your right to own your own private nuclear arsenal?"

"Why do so many people have only one name?" Sacher reflected. "After all, one needs a different name for every persona, and maybe even several names for the same persona."

"And why," Zeko chimed, "aren't there more people with no names at all? After all, many of them have no personalities!"

"Zeko," I reproved her.

Sacher: "Why are there so many answers all the time, and so few good questions?"

"But it's OK, we can help," Zeko came to the rescue. "We have more good questions."

10

A Trip to the Bahamas

Café Bombshell evidently became an instant hit, or so the rabbits told us. They told us about all the expensive decor, about their lavish shows, about the occasional fashion shows they staged ("for the well-dressed rabbit"), and, of course, about the drink specials. They even brought home a sample menu which, under the heading "Today's specials", listed the following drinks:

The Munich Agreement (carrot juice, champagne, apricot brandy): If Chamberlain had only offered Hitler one of these at Munich, Hitler might have forgotten all about Sudetenland.

The Fall of Rome (vodka, gin, kahlua, Frangelico): Good thing they didn't have this drink in ancient Rome. The city would have fallen a lot sooner.

The Lessons of Vietnam (vegetable juice, kiwi wine, melon liqueur): You'll be drawing lessons after you drink this one.

World War Two (We give it everything we've got -- literally): Reliving World War Two would be easier than the day after this drink. Got a talkative friend? Would you prefer peace and quiet? Buy your friend this drink. Nothing like a good war to produce a bit of peace and quiet.

The Gang of Four (scotch, bourbon, rye whiskey, grenadine): They started with liking the same drink and ended with anti-state conspiracy. It could happen to you too. Drink with caution. Parental supervision recommended. Waiver required.

The Soviet-Polish Treaty of Friendship & Cooperation (slivovitsa, vodka, strawberry juice): They drank ample quantities of this concoction before signing the agreement. See for yourself what you will sign after about eight of these!

All of this sounded very interesting, and Kris and I at once expressed interest in coming to the Club to see it for ourselves. To our disappointment, the rabbits put us off.

Sacher: "We should install the velvet curtains first."

Zeko: "Tonight is Rabbits Only Night. You can't come tonight."

Sacher: "The Club is closed tonight for redecorating. We're installing some beautiful marble columns that we just imported from Florence, also some fabulous jade pottery, 16th century Chinese, I believe."

Zeko: "I don't have time to talk right now. I am busy planning the next month's entertainment."

And so it went. No matter what we said or did, we just couldn't get them to take us to Café Bombshell. But they did not spare the stories. From everything we heard it seemed clear that the rabbits were very successful with their new venture. They told us about their platinum-plated limousine (complete with chauffeur), about the exorbitant attire they had purchased (but conveniently stashed away at the Club), and about the special osmanthus tree-lined access road which they were having constructed to provide a dramatic approach to Café Bombshell. All of this was, of course, a pleasant change from all the adventure stories to which we had been subjected not so long before. It encouraged us to hope that the rabbits would be content to settle down as safe, middle-of-the-road business-rabbits.

I will confess to some disappointment that they never invited us to come for a ride in their limousine, never took us sailing in their 150-ft. cruise-boat, never even took us out to the peacock sanctuary that they said they had opened somewhere on the edge of town. But of course, our successful business-rabbits were very busy, with many important things to do.

In August we had some excitement, occasioned by Kris's need to go to Seoul, South Korea, to obtain a new visa. Now it might seem strange to you that the Japanese did not want to issue their own visas in their own country. But I think this was the fruit of the Japanese-South Korean Friendship Society. They cooked up a scheme under which foreigners (*gaijin*) wanting to stay in Japan had to obtain their papers in Korea, and those wanting to stay in Korea, had to obtain their visas in Japan. This way there was a guaranteed injection of cash into the airline industry and local hotels on both sides. So Kris, wanting to stay in Japan, was busy packing her things, when Sacher showed up bedside.

"I want to come along too," Sacher announced.

"But you don't need a visa. Only humans are required to get such things, not stuffed rabbits," Kris explained.

"No, I want to come," Sacher insisted, with a grin on her face.

"Are you going to pay for your own ticket?" Kris asked.

"Oh come now. I'm a stuffed rabbit, as you seem to have forgotten. I travel for free. It's one of the many many privileges enjoyed by stuffed animals (unless their humans decide to imprison them in the luggage, of course). I'll sit on your lap."

"Why thank you, Sacher, but are you sure you wouldn't prefer to ride in the baggage," Kris said, teasing her stuffed companion.

"Oh dreadful! We tried that last time and hated every moment. If we hadn't had our glow-in-the-dark playing cards on hand, we would have been totally bored."

"All right," said Kris, finally giving in. "You can sit on my lap...provided you help me pack."

For my own part, I didn't see Sacher helping much with the packing. But come departure time, there were Sacher and Kris, hand-in-paw, lining up for tickets. Zeko and I stayed home.

Now, much as I missed Kris during the three days she was gone, I had at least looked forward to some earnest heart-to-heart conversations with Zeko. But do you think she would talk to me? No. On the contrary, she spent the entire time sitting on the pillow in the bedroom, staring at the wall. How utterly boring! Anyone would have thought she was just a stuffed rabbit! I was reduced to watching Japanese television, most of which was in a language I didn't even understand. But there was one thing I did understand -- that strange commercial, broadcast in English, the second night that they were gone. I was sitting on the couch, rereading G. W. F. Hegel's *Phenomenology of the Mind*, enjoying the soothing effect of Hegel's ruminations about the bacchanalian revel in which no one is sober, when a televised commercial penetrated my consciousness:

First lady: "Grenda, I thought you were going out with Rucy for lunch."
Grenda: "No, Ginger, I changed my mind. Rucy has the most awful brain decay you've ever seen. And when she smiles, it's just awful."
Ginger: "Doesn't she brush?"
Grenda: "I don't think so. She certainly doesn't floss."
Ginger: "Well, I must say your brain positively glows. What brand of brain paste do you use?"
Grenda: "Who me? Oh, I use Crano-Glow brain paste -- it makes all the colors glow."
Authoritative male voice: "Yes, folks, Crano-Glow brain paste can make the difference between sanity and insanity. Visit your pharmacy today and ask for Crano-Glow. Accept no substitutes."

I got up off the couch and turned the television off, but it was hard to continue to read Hegel after having absorbed that message about brain paste. I leafed through the index to *The Phenomenology of Mind*, in search of an entry for "paste, brain"...but there was nothing. Maybe they didn't have brain paste in Hegel's day.

At any rate, after three days of stoney silence on Zeko's part, Kris and Sacher returned, and I learned the truth about Sacher's interest in visiting Seoul.

"Do you know what Sacher did in Korea?" Kris asked for openers. Of course I had no idea. "Apparently she was on a secret assignment, and needed to track down a fellow eco-terrorist known only as 'the goat', who was spending some time in Pyongyang."

"I've heard of this goat," I replied. "It's been on the evening news. He's a dangerous fellow."

"Was he behind the destruction of the clock tower in Fargo?" Kris asked.

"It was never conclusively proven, but I think so," I replied. "But I also read, in last month's issue of *The Unknown Threat,* that 'the goat' is in cahoots with a group of brain surgeons. Apparently the brain surgeons plan to take out people's brains in towns earmarked for terrorist action. That way the response will be limp. If 'the goat' was in Pyongyang, then that is serious business. What else did Sacher say?"

"Ask her."

"That stuff about the goat working with the brain surgeons – that is a tapestry of lies," Sacher explained. "We are on the same side. In fact, we were chased at one point by local brain surgeons and had to disguise ourselves as palm trees in order to elude them."

"This is sounding better all the time," I remarked, with barely concealed sarcasm.

"And just when we thought there was no threat to our domestic tranquility."

"So Sacher left you alone in Seoul and spent the entire time in Pyongyang?" I asked.

"No," Kris answered. "She spent only a day in Pyongyang. She got home late that night, and on our last morning, as I was doing my best to fit in a few Buddhist temples and secret gardens on the way to the airport, Sacher made time to dash out to a large store dealing in bootlegged weaponry in downtown Seoul."

"Oh good!" screamed Zeko with delight, as they contemplated another terrorist binge. "You got there!"

"I did indeed," said Sacher, grinning from ear to ear.

So our rabbits were up to their old tricks again. Well, at least they weren't destroying anything in town. But despite her elation over the bootlegged weapons, Zeko was still pouting. Zeko, it seemed, had wanted to go along too, but someone had to stay home and keep me company.

"You got to go to Pyongyang," Zeko pointed out to Sacher, with a hint of reproach in her voice. "So I get a vacation too."

"But Zeko," Sacher answered. "You know it wasn't a vacation. It was a business trip."

"It doesn't matter. I want a vacation. I want to go to the Bahamas."

Zeko has a way with all of us. There is just no resisting her. In fact, the rabbits immediately began packing their suitcases for their trip to the Bahamas. I think they would have left then and there, but we persuaded them to stay for dinner. But they left first thing the following morning. Zeko called the taxi company, whose cabs, as I noticed, were all emblazoned with the image of a smiling rabbit. The last thing I heard Zeko say as they got into the taxi was "To the Bahamas, and step on it." And the taxi sped away.

The last thing I heard Zeko say as they got into the taxi was "To the Bahamas, and step on it." And the taxi sped away.

The rabbits were gone for two weeks. We missed them terribly, but eventually, they pulled up at the apartment building, in the very same taxi as before.

The rabbits had their version of what had happened. According to them, they had taken the taxi all the way to the Bahamas and back. When Kris and I suggested that maybe they also took a plane or a boat, they glared at us and asked, "What are you, some sort of primitives? We went by taxi! That's it!" And they showed us the receipt for the taxi fare: $16,495 roundtrip. Now I had noticed that their fur seemed a little bleached, which *might*, of course, mean that they had been out in the sun. But they might just as easily have made a few visits to a sun-lamp tanning parlor within the city limits of Sapporo.

In fact, Kris and I were skeptical at first. We were not inclined to believe they had been to the Bahamas at all, whether by taxi or by plane. But then they told us about the clocks in the Bahamas, how they have dials but no hands, because in the Bahamas it is always anytime you want. Now it seemed to us that this is not the sort of thing you just make up. No, they must have really gone to the Bahamas. By taxi. Who knows how they did it?

They even made a side trip to Bermuda, with the same taxi, and dined at Bermuda's fabled San Giorgio Ristorante.

The Bahamas trip did them a lot of good. They both insisted on wearing sunglasses everywhere for about three weeks after their return, even though the weather was mostly overcast in Sapporo. And for about the same time-span, they had these rather mindless grins on their faces all the time.

11

Whistling Alligators

One day, John and Vera, two friends of ours, stopped by on an impromptu visit. Zeko and Sacher were sitting on the couch watching a video they had purchased, "Captain Stubb's Survival Guide." Captain Stubb wore a field jacket, with binoculars strapped around his neck, and had a corn-cob pipe stuffed in his mouth. He talked endlessly about what to do when one is in the wilderness in "enemy territory." The odd thing was that he was using downtown Bellevue for a backdrop. Vera immediately spied the rabbits and declared, "Oh, what nice stuffed rabbits!"

"We only look stuffed because you don't know us yet," Sacher snapped at her, I thought a bit rudely. "If you knew us better, we wouldn't look so stuffed."

Now Sacher said all of this in a very loud voice, but to our great surprise, neither John nor Vera seemed to hear Sacher.

Nor did they hear Zeko when she barked, "Nobody asked you to visit! We're busy!" Maybe our friends are hard of hearing, I thought to myself.

Certain now that they could only hear someone if they were positively shouted at, I raised my voice and shrieked, "So what are you two up to today?"

Well, John and Vera seemed to fall backwards a little now. Evidently, they were not *that* hard of hearing. "You don't have to shout," said John, regaining his composure. "We're not deaf."

"If they were deaf, no amount of shouting would make any difference anyway," Zeko pointed out to me.

"That doesn't help matters," I cautioned Zeko.

"So you would rather we were deaf!" Vera asked stiffly.

"No, of course not -- "

"We would just rather you were not here!" said Sacher.

"Don't listen to them," Kris advised. "They're just babbling."

Somehow John and Vera misunderstood this, and started to go. "We don't have to stay," John said, as they moved toward the door.

"You certainly don't!" Sacher agreed.

"Don't let the rabbits throw you out!" I pleaded, finally managing to get a word in. "Just ignore them!"

"You mean your stuffed rabbits?" Vera asked. "But we *were* ignoring them." She picked up Sacher.

"Put me down! Put me down! Pick on someone your own size!" Sacher screamed, to no avail.

"You didn't hear that?" I asked, I guess a bit naively.

"Oh yes, sure," Vera said, humoring me. "Your rabbit said, 'I love you, Vera,'"

"Don't get your hopes up too high, Vera," Sacher said to this.

We tried to explain the rabbits to John and Vera, who seemed especially interested that the rabbits had been assigned to file reports on us. They wanted to see this Café Bombshell, but I had to explain that even we hadn't seen it, and that we didn't even know precisely where it was, although we suspected that it was somewhere in Sus'kino.

After they left, I reproached the rabbits. "How could you embarrass us like that?"

"Like *what?*" Sacher asked innocently. "It seems to me that they were not troubled by anything *we* said."

"Now look, you two," Kris said. "We've got you two figured out. You're some sort of magical rabbits and only we can hear you, right?"

"Not necessarily," Zeko advised. "Hearing improves with practice."

"Well, it doesn't improve very fast, from what we can see. And if you're going to insist on not being heard by our friends, maybe you can at least keep quiet when they visit, so that we don't have to make fools of ourselves."

"We can certainly understand your dilemma," Sacher said in an almost avuncular tone of voice. (What's a female rabbit doing sounding avuncular, anyway?) "That reminds me of the time we foiled a band of wicked terrorists who had taken over a chocolate factory in Lyon..."

"That reminds me," Zeko responded, "of the time I was being pursued by the terrorists across the fourth and fifth bridges over the Arno. If I had not demolished those bridges, using special high-tech explosives I had obtained from a private source in Morocco, who knows how many people might have been hurt! It was in Casablanca, in fact..."

"That reminds me of the first time I saw *Casablanca*, oh Humphrey Bogart was just great," Sacher said.

"That reminds me of the ninth time I saw *Lawrence of Arabia* and my mind was wandering and I started thinking about *Casablanca*," Zeko reminisced, adding quickly: "I was sitting in the sixth row, next to the aisle."

"Rabbits! Let's not do the reminiscences bit again, OK?"

"It's time for my nap," Sacher observed.

"Mine too," said Zeko.

Seconds later, they were snoring loudly.

When the rabbits awoke after several hours of napping, they starting working furiously on the calendar for Café Bombshell.

"Next week we have scheduled a troupe of very talented geese," Sacher told us. "They will perform Beethoven's Symphony No. 9."

"You mean the geese can play all the instruments?" I asked.

"Don't be so silly," Zeko corrected me. "They sing it while tap-dancing. It's the tap-dancing version of Beethoven's Ninth."

"And the week after, we will have the Royal Highland Bagpipe band playing the bagpipe version of the Mozart Requiem," Sacher explained. "That will be in an arrangement for 20 bagpipes."

"And then the week after that we will have Lily the Lemur on the banjo, performing her own transcription-for-banjo of Mahler's Symphony of a Thousand. It will be great," Zeko cooed, displaying vast contentment.

"One minute," Kris said. "Mahler's Symphony of a Thousand is called that because it requires a thousand performers, including several choirs. And you're going to have it performed in a reduction for solo banjo!"

"Of course," Sacher replied jovially. "We think it will be a big improvement. And besides, we don't have room in the Club for a thousand performers."

"But you don't have to perform Mahler either," I pointed out.

"Mahler is worth hearing, including in a transcription for banjo," Sacher observed with an air of sagacity.

"And then," Zeko continued, "we are negotiating to have a special performance of Mussorgsky's *Pictures at an Exhibition* put on by a team of African elephants in conjunction with the Metropolitan Museum of Art. The elephants will perform the music while museum staff display suitable pictures."

"We think it will be a big hit," Sacher said, obviously enthralled. "But we are having some headaches with the Whistling Alligators. We have scheduled and rescheduled them five times and they keep canceling."

"Why don't you just forget about them, then?" Kris suggested.

"Are you kidding??!" Zeko asked with a look of wild indignation and arched her eyebrows. "The Whistling Alligators offer a unique program of best loved melodies by Stephen Collins Foster and Schubert *Lieder*. Who else will offer 'Way Down upon the Swanee River' and 'Ach, Schmerz!' on the same program? They even perform a disco version of 'Tamo daleko.' Not only that, but they do a whistle-along routine. By the end of the evening, the customers are guaranteed to be going home whistling the tunes. No! We *need* them!"

"That reminds me of the time I visited Spain..." I started.

"Don't try to play that trick on us," Sacher advised. "We invented it."

12

Are You Normal?

"**A**re you normal?" Zeko asked me one day when Kris was out, purchasing some cleaning materials. This was the first time that Zeko was talking to me privately -- I mean in Kris's absence. "You and Kris -- are you normal?"

"Huh?" I grunted, at my most inarticulate.

"Are you *nor-mal?*" Zeko drew out the last word for emphasis.

"What is this -- an interrogation?"

"Well," Zeko pressed me, as if she were entitled to an answer.

"Yes, I suppose we're pretty normal."

"Good."

"What's good about it?" I asked.

"Well, we were hoping you two would fit the bill. We've advertised the film under the title, *Normal Life.*"

"*What* film?" I asked with some concern.

"We're going to show a film at Café Bombshell, to enlighten and amuse our customers. About normal life."

"Something your customers don't know anything about, I take it."

"You don't have to get so smart."

"So what do you plan to do, film us around the house?"

"Yes. We thought we would capture the essence of normal life, showing you two eating breakfast, sleeping together, shopping for groceries, watching the evening news hour, that sort of thing."

"Will this film of yours have a plot of some kind?"

"Does your life?" Zeko asked, largely rhetorically.

"No, not really. It just sort of flows along."

"Well, that's what we want for our film!"

"But it will bore your customers to death. And where did you get this idea anyway? From watching old Andy Warhol flicks?"

"There are just too many weird movies around nowadays, and we wanted to make a nice normal sort of film. So the subject of normal life seemed like just what we needed. And besides, some of our customers are interested in the mating practices of humans."

"Look, Zeko," I said firmly. "I don't think this interests me. Don't you understand the notion of privacy? You are invading our privacy."

None of my reservations made much impression on Zeko, who noted that human nature-lovers have frequently filmed animals engaged in rather private behavior, and that evening, as Kris and I were retiring, the rabbits started hauling out various cameras, lights, and other equipment, and setting it up. "Now don't forget to smile for the camera," Zeko advised us. Needless to say, we hustled the rabbits out of our bedroom without much ado, and got their film equipment out of the room too. What nerve!

But the rabbits were not so easily deterred. The next morning, as we opened the bedroom door and stumbled out groggily, here were Zeko and Sacher behind the camera, filming. "Damn rabbits!" Kris muttered and went into the kitchen to put on the coffee. They filmed us as we stumbled around trying to wake up. They filmed us as we had our morning coffee. They filmed us as we made breakfast and ate it. Despite her intent concentration, Zeko was in a chatty mood. As ever.

"I had a dream last night," Zeko began.

"I'm sure it was very important," Sacher offered.

"I think so, yes, very important," Zeko replied without waiting for any reaction from us. "I dreamt that Sacher and I kidnapped some space aliens and performed physical exams on *them!*"

"That's a reversal of sorts," Kris observed.

"Except that they all turned out to be very normal," Zeko continued, with an air of disappointment. "They were just like us, they were even stuffed with polyester fibers."

"Well, that's what you like, isn't it?" I commented. "Normal life!"

Sacher had something to say. When Sacher had something to say, it was inevitably important. So, as she straightened herself up and took a deep breath, we all instinctively faced toward her. Finally, Sacher came out with it: "I'm not so sure that you two are normal. I think this first needs to be established."

"Maybe you could just find someone else to film? Some couple that you feel confident is normal," I suggested.

"There are some advantages associated with living here, with our subjects," Sacher observed wisely. "But it might be sensible to give you two a short test first, to see if you are normal."

"What if we refuse to take the test," said Kris, slipping into automatic rebellion.

"Oh, let's not think about worst-case scenarios," Sacher replied, charming as ever. "Here's the first question. Do you think there is life on Planet Xypon?"

"No, and I don't think there is a Planet Xypon either," Kris answered in what the rabbits could only have taken as an uncooperative tone of voice.

"That's not one of your options," Sacher pointed out. "It's a simple yes-no question, not an essay question. OK, here's question number 2: Do you think there is life on Planet Earth?"

"What kind of dumb question is that?" I asked.

"Just answer the question," Zeko prompted. "Yes or no."

"No," I answered, as I was starting to feel like being uncooperative myself.

"*Abnormal!*" the rabbits chimed in unison, looking at each other.

"OK, here's your third and last question. What do you think of travel by submarine?"

"This is a yes or no question, right?"

Kris and I looked at each other and smiled with mild amusement. But Zeko was getting impatient and started tapping the table. "No opinion, no views, never thought of it, eh?" Zeko muttered with evident impatience. "What kind of people are you anyway?"

"*Normal* people, remember?" Kris offered.

"I don't think so," replied Zeko decisively. "Submarine travel is safe, elegant, comfortable, fast. You can go anywhere by submarine. On our submarine, for example, we have sumptuous purple and crimson satin cushions with gold braid, finely woven Andorran wool carpets; we also have a quartet of harpists who play Debussy and Faure and Scriabin on the harp."

I thought it was significant that they started by describing the "creature comforts" aboard their submarine. But both of them became very animated now, and seemed to forget all about their "test". They wanted to talk about their submarine. We learned now that it was a platinum-plated submarine, that it had no periscope, that having been replaced with the latest echographic sensors. We also learned that they had a fully equipped mini-theater on board, and enjoyed watching old Tom Mix westerns from the silent era, and Ava Gardner movies ("She's the best!" as Zeko put it). The rabbits also claimed that they were routinely driving to work in town, in their submarine, driving under the streets to avoid traffic. Neither Kris nor I could imagine that a submarine would be very effective underground. But it didn't seem worthwhile to pursue this question. And besides, we didn't want to seem any more "abnormal" than we evidently already did. But between the two of us, we were quite convinced that all this talk of a submarine with satin cushions and harpists, traveling below the streets of Sapporo, was a lot of bunk.

One day, about two weeks later, when I had largely put all of this out of my mind, I was walking down Rabbit Street, one of the main boulevards in the North District of Sapporo. All of a sudden I noticed the street bulging, as if something were pushing up from below. I stopped in my tracks, more curious than anything else. Other people were watching too. Meanwhile, this bulge was getting bigger, the road was forming a small hill, and then suddenly, the surface noisily broke apart, and, to my delight, I saw a beautiful platinum-plated submarine rise up, glistening in the sunlight. For a moment nothing else happened. Then the hatch opened, and here were our two stuffed rabbits, looking around with confusion.

"Zeko, I told you that this was not the right way," Sacher berated her comrade. It was the first time I had ever heard Sacher criticize Zeko.

"But the echographic monitors showed that we were home," Zeko replied defensively. "How was I to know that someone had hit the memory switch and that we were looking at a playback of yesterday's docking?"

"So you think I had something to do with this?" asked Sacher in a tough tone of voice.

The rabbits' submarine had emerged through the street, and the rabbits were looking around in confusion.

"I'm not saying anything except that it was not my fault," Zeko pleaded.

Zeko had a chance to repeat that line again later, because inevitably, the police got to the scene very fast. Poor rabbits. Here they were being led away on charges of obstructing traffic, illegal parking, and wanton destruction of public property. These charges seemed pretty vague to me, but I suppose that lawmakers never bothered to make laws specifically aimed at barring submarines from public streets.

I suppose it's not that surprising that these two rabbit-eco-terrorists should find themselves behind bars. The irony was, of course, that they were in jail now not for fighting polluters and anti-life capitalists but, as the official charges delicately put it, for "the wanton destruction of public property." Maybe that's not so different.

I accompanied the rabbits, hoping that I could help in some way. But -- and I should have expected this -- they did not need my help at all. They were behind bars for all of 32 minutes. I counted. They were allowed one phone call, which they made to the Chief Prosecutor. He came over in a flash, all smiles, immediately ordered the charges dropped and the rabbits released. He and the rabbits then started talking amiably. They were, it turned out, big friends. I suspect, although I have no evidence, that the Prosecutor was on the rabbits' "payroll". The Prosecutor then invited the three of us back to his office, a luxurious, spacious office with a veritable art museum in one section of the room, and a full bar in another. We sat around and had drinks. And before I knew what was happening, here was the Prosecutor offering to arrange to have the sewers refitted in order to make their submarine travel easier. Here was a lesson.

The three of us got back late that night. In the excitement, I had forgotten to call Kris, who had been pacing around nervously, wondering what had happened to all of us and sponging down the light fixtures and the walls in an effort to calm her nerves. She was more than a little relieved to have us back safe and sound.

We slept soundly that night and, on getting up the following morning, found the two rabbits sitting in the living room, watching a video playback of sections of our nocturnal slumber. Here, for all the world to see, was documented evidence that I snore, at least on occasion. Normal life.

13

Brain Surgeons
at the Club

Fortunately for Kris and myself, the rabbits soon found a new distraction and quickly forgot all about "Normal Life". It had been raining for a few days when Sacher went to the video rental store and returned with a video of the unabridged, unexpurgated version of Ingmar Bergman's "The Seventh Seal". Zeko and Sacher watched it with great interest. Kris and I even joined them. It was fun to see that old classic once again, especially the chess match with Death. But I was a little surprised to find the rabbits rewatching "The Seventh Seal" the following morning, and even more surprised when, upon returning from work that day, I found them still watching "The Seventh Seal". "So how many times do you two plan to watch that film?" I asked them.

"Is it any of your business?" Zeko replied curtly.

"We like the film," added Sacher somewhat more diplomatically. "It gives us ideas."

I was soon to discover just what sort of ideas Sacher meant, for by the next day, they were no longer watching and rewatching the film per se, but only the short flagellant sequence, in which a group of about 30 so-called "flagellants" crawled through the town on their knees, at the same time whipping themselves on their backs with all the strength they could apply. Through all of this, they were wailing to the heavens and singing "Dies Irae" to a march tempo. At the front of this procession of flagellants two monks swung incense (one of them being left-handed); another monk carried a small shrine. And there were two large crucifixes, each borne by several monks. The entire sequence, including a homily in the middle, lasted about 4 minutes and 15 seconds.

But the rabbits watched it intently, running it forwards, then in reverse at double-speed, then forwards again, then in reverse, and so on, ad nauseam.

"So this is it?!" I challenged them.

"This is an important scene," Sacher pointed out to me helpfully. "Notice the dusty road, the wooden gate through which they pass, the gabled house standing unpretentiously in the background, and the pine trees in the distance."

"Those are elm trees," Zeko corrected her.

"I thought they were pine trees; they look like pine trees to me."

"Let's rewind it and watch it again. You'll see: they're elm trees."

"You're not going to convince me that that's all you find interesting in this sequence," I replied.

"We enjoy watching these people whip themselves," said Zeko very defiantly. "It is instructive."

Then silence. The rabbits were watching the scene with intent rapture. I gave up and went into the kitchen, where I found Kris drinking warm milk. I poured myself a glass of Cal Pis and then sat down at the table with Kris. I told her about the rabbits and we talked for a while about them. I gulped down my Cal Pis, poured myself a second glass, and quaffed that too. Eventually Kris and I went back out to the living room. The rabbits were no longer watching the film: they were acting it out. Here was Sacher, crawling on her knees, while flagellating herself with an improvised leather whip. Zeko was, of course, marching in front carrying a cross. How did I know that Sacher would end up having to do the flagellation? Sacher was singing some sort of song, no doubt her best imitation of what she thought she had heard on the film. But for the life of me, it didn't sound like anything specific. Kris and I looked at each other, sighed deeply, rolled our eyes, and went back into the kitchen.

They carried on like this until about 10 p.m. when, of course, it was time for them to go to the Café. When they returned the next morning, however, they seemed very different. They just sat at the coffee table, staring at each other rather blankly.

"What's wrong?" Kris asked them, sensing trouble.

"Oh, trouble," Sacher mumbled.

"Come on, share your troubles," Kris coaxed them.

"It's the brain surgeons," Sacher mumbled.

"It's the lousy rotten stinking brain surgeons!" Zeko screamed at the top of her lungs. "They're wrecking everything!"

"Of course, the brain surgeons," I replied. "I've been noticing that they were up to something."

"It's awful. They are coming to our club in droves, wearing their blue gowns, with mirrors strapped onto their heads," Sacher explained.

"Are they bad tippers or something?" Kris wondered.

"No, they tip generously," Sacher replied. "They just make trouble."

"Like what?" I pressed Sacher.

"They are running around promoting brain surgery as if it were candy," Sacher revealed. "They make conversation with our other customers and then, after they establish a rapport, they deliver the hard pitch. They have all kinds of gimmicks too. Buy one brain surgery, get a second one free: invite a friend. Or -- want to try something different? try brain surgery. Or -- try our express brain surgery: the entire procedure during your lunch hour! These miscreants even lure customers with prattle about the comfortable gurneys and pillows available for brain surgery patients."

Kris was snickering. "It's not a laughing matter," Zeko snapped.

"But surely your customers aren't taking this stuff seriously! Are they?" Kris asked.

"We have had about eight weasels who have had brain surgery since all this began," Sacher continued. Zeko just sat there with a scowl on her face.

"You're not letting weasels in, are you?" I asked.

"Their money is as good as anyone else's."

"But they smell funny," I pointed out.

"OK, they smell a little funny. But they are very witty, and make the most hilarious jokes. They just crack me up. And they like to drink expensive umbrella drinks. But not after brain surgery. The post-surgical weasels just drift into the club like they're in some sort of trance and sit down, with the most vacant look on their faces. And once they've had brain surgery, the only thing they ever order is lemon water."

"Sounds like a cheap drink."

"It is! But it gets worse," Sacher continued. "They don't make any more jokes, they don't react to other animals' jokes, they hardly even talk except in a slow plodding hollow monotone. Most of the time they just stare vacantly ahead of themselves."

"It sounds like lobotomy."

"Well, of course," Sacher said. "And lobotomy is bad news. Not only that. But if we start getting too many lobotomized weasels sitting around in the club, business will start to fall off."

"Why not enforce a dress code? No surgeons in blue gowns," I offered.

"I think it will take more than that to deal with the problem," Sacher replied.

"Who's behind all of this?" asked Kris.

"'The Fat One' and his lackeys," Sacher admitted. "We think they want to destroy our business. You're right about them. They are, in fact, hooked up as part of the international brain surgeon-polluter-exploiter anti-life conspiracy."

"Just who is 'the Fat One'?" I asked. "I haven't heard of him."

"He is the king of the exploiters, he and his family own stock in all the major pollutant enterprises, including the Arc of Splendour, and he has been working with the brain surgeons as part of a vast international conspiracy."

"Throw them out!" I suggested. "Don't you have bouncers?"

"We tried that," Sacher noted. "But the next night, the bouncers in question returned, and looked like they had had brain surgery."

"It's out of control, out of control!" Zeko screamed suddenly. "It's all out of control! We have to do something!!"

"It does sound desperate," I readily conceded, as I grew steadily more concerned myself.

"We have a very fine friend, a wise old crow, who lives in the birch trees at the Botanical Gardens. Zeko and I will go to see him and ask his advice."

"What's his name?" I asked.

"Giuseppe. He's Italian."

"What's an Italian crow doing in Sapporo?" Kris asked.

"What are *we* doing here? What are any of us doing here? Giuseppe sings in the local opera. That's why you can always hear him crowing away, reciting his part."

The rabbits, it turned out, had even made an appointment to see this crow. Evidently, Giuseppe had a very busy calendar, and the rabbits had to wait four days before Giuseppe could make time for them. Those four days were just agonizing. The rabbits seemed very agitated. They even started having heavily armed bodyguards -- four rhinos, to be exact -- follow them around at close quarters. Needless to say, when the rabbits came into our kitchen, it got a bit crowded with the rhinos and all. All of us waited impatiently for the time to pass.

14

"Brain Surgeons on Parade"

The rabbits had obtained an appointment for the first Wednesday in November, and for the first time in our experience, invited us to come along. We decided to make a picnic of it, and took along a large beach towel and two baskets full of goodies. Early November is a wonderful time for autumn colors in Sapporo, and the trees at the Botanical Gardens were ablaze with glory. The leaves were diverse shades of red, flaming yellow, golden orange, warm brown, and various shades of green.

The rabbits knew exactly where we needed to go and marched ahead, unable to restrain themselves. The rabbits set quite a pace, and Kris and I, carrying the baskets, hurried to keep up. We crossed a lush meadow and approached a large birch tree. The rabbits looked up, fixed their gaze on a rather large and utterly mangy-looking crow and declared triumphantly, "That's Giuseppe!"

Kris and I cooperatively spread the towel on the ground near this tree, and started to unpack the baskets. The rabbits were hopping around with unconcealed glee.

"Beautiful, such melody, such a fine voice," said Sacher, sighing in utter rapture.

"What?" asked Kris.

"Giuseppe's singing, of course," Zeko interjected.

Giuseppe sat on the uppermost limb of the tree, and in a raucous monotone, repeated, seemingly endlessly, "Caw, caw, caw! Caw, caw, caw!"

"Yeah," I said, "caw, caw, caw!" I grinned.

"What are you, tone-deaf?" Zeko asked. "Don't you recognize it? It's 'La Donna è mobile' from Verdi's *Rigoletto!*"

"It's beautiful," Sacher sighed.

"Caw, caw, caw! Caw, caw, caw!"

Kris and I couldn't hear what the rabbits heard. But we didn't say anything and quietly unpacked lunch. "Would you like something to drink, you two?" Kris asked the rabbits.

But they were checking their watches and, as if struck by the second-hand, suddenly dashed for the tree full-speed, and climbed up the branches with a skill I did not know rabbits possessed. The rabbits soon reached Giuseppe, and we could see them exchanging warm greetings. The rabbits pointed down to us, and Giuseppe spread his wings in greeting. We waved. Then the three began to converse earnestly. We couldn't hear the rabbits from where we were, but we could hear Giuseppe loud and clear: "Caw, caw, caw! Caw, caw, caw!" The rabbits listened carefully with cocked ears, nodding with reverence. Finally, Giuseppe flew off, perhaps to another consultation, or more likely to take part in the afternoon rehearsal at the Sapporo Opera House.

The rabbits descended more gingerly than they had gone up. Both of them seemed to be thinking deeply about Giuseppe's advice. As they approached where we were sitting, Kris asked, "So did you get some good advice?"

"Yes, excellent advice!" Sacher said, grinning broadly.

"It sounded to me like Giuseppe just continued to sing 'La Donna è mobile'," I cracked.

"Oh, don't show your musical ignorance," Sacher advised. After a short pause, she asked, "Why don't you two eat your lunch?"

What had the rabbits been advised to do? Giuseppe had some highly original advice for them, a plan that neither Kris nor I would have thought of. He had suggested that they stage an opera, sung in Italian. Giuseppe proposed to prepare the libretto for them. The opera would be titled, "Brain Surgeons on Parade!"

Having lived with the rabbits for a while, Kris and I were no longer so easily surprised by their various schemes. But I will admit that neither of us had a clue as to how staging an Italian opera was going to solve their problems with the brain surgeons.

For the next two weeks, the apartment was abuzz with excitement as the rabbits prepared for the big day. We saw some of the enormous posters they had prepared. We marveled at some of the costumes for the extravaganza, which the rabbits, in their graciousness, deigned to hang in our closet. When the big evening arrived, the rabbits donned operatic capes and marched downstairs to their submarine. Kris and I wanted so much to go along. But the rabbits advised against it. So we sat up in bed as the sub's solar-powered engine started to roar. Then, we heard the usual blast and rumble as the submarine tore out of its underground harbor and made for Café Bombshell.

Kris and I were so excited that we could not sleep. We just lay there staring at the ceiling muttering to ourselves, from time to time, "I wonder how everything is going at the Club," and "I hope things work out for the rabbits." Finally, about 8:43 a.m., the rabbits floated in, more or less, their faces lit up with the self-satisfied glow of triumph and deep contentment.

"I guess everything went well," I noted.

"We've been awake all night," Kris added. "We couldn't sleep."

"I know," Sacher replied.

"Well, well,...do we get a story?" I said. I was desperate to hear how the evening had gone.

The rabbits told us the story from start to finish. How they put on this extraordinary Italian opera in the grand style. How the Club was packed. The peacocks were there, strutting their stuff and unfurling their plumage. The goats were there, a bit self-conscious about their lack of schooling, and doing their best to look urbane and cosmopolitan. The penguins were there. They have nothing to hide, and kept flapping their wings noisily every time there was a funny line in the opera. The silver hatchet fish were also there, as usual swimming in their drinks. A few caribou were in attendance as well, although they evidently found the café's chairs most uncomfortable and kept squirming in their seats, trying to find a more comfortable position. And the weasels were there, many of the poor things with utterly vacant expressions. And yes, the brain surgeons were also there. The surgeons were very boisterous when they arrived and all sat together at one long table. Some of them sat upside down. OK, it wasn't really sitting. They were more or less standing on their heads. And they kept complaining to the Club's waitresses that the bubbles in their drinks were going the wrong way, and they wanted the bubbles *reversed*.

It just so happened that the Club retained two world-renowned physicists on its staff. The rabbits wouldn't tell us their names, but left us with the suspicion that they were No-bel-Prize winners. These two physicists lost no time in devis-ing a special motorized translucent drinking vessel equipped with miniscule pipes blowing bubbles heavier than liquid into the drink. The result was that the bubbles gradually fizzed to-ward the bottom of the glass, until they reached a certain criti-cal mass. Then there was a small explosion -- "Really only a very small explosion," as Sacher put it -- and the entire drink fogged up and turned a deep murky yellow. Then seconds later, it faded into a cola-like color, and the process began again. This drink made a big hit with the brain surgeons, of course, and pretty soon, all of them were ordering the same, the Bubble Down Special, even the brain surgeons who were not standing on their heads.

Then the big moment arrived, the curtain pulled back, and the production began. Evidently Giuseppe himself, with his fine tenor voice, played the part of chief surgeon in this combination farce and exposé. Three very talented cows per-formed some impressive crooning that left much of the audi-ence in tears. A chorus of marmosets played the nursing staff. These marmoset-nurses cocked their heads back, clutched clip-boards against their breasts, and hurried back and forth, looking very busy and very important. The whole time they sang a refrain about unnecessary operations and unnecessary surgeons. But the hit of the evening was the hyena, who played the part of the patient. His aria, "You cut me up!", mesmer-ized the audience, driving the brain surgeons to frenzy, and by the end of the evening, the whole audience was singing,

When I feel a little blue
and my spirit cracks with pain
You're always there to tell me
It's a problem with my brain!
You want to cut inside and see

What makes me want to pout.
Whatever it is your answer is
You want to cut it out!
You cut me up!
You cut me up!
You want to cut inside and see
You want to cut it out!

Even the brain-dead weasels joined in the singing, and as the evening drew to an end, the rabbits saw that all the brain surgeons were now standing on their heads and were sobbing violently, their tears running across their foreheads and into their hair. They all felt remorse and started shouting how they didn't mean any harm, and how they wouldn't perform any more unnecessary lobotomies. In a gesture of good faith, they even elected a Board of Commissioners, consisting entirely of owls of Minerva -- the ones with the rotating heads – which they promised would supervise their surgery.

Toward the end of the evening, one of the brain surgeons who had been sitting to one side stood up, and tore off his scrub, to reveal a checkered red and white headscarf. When he tore off his blue surgeon gown, revealing a flowing Arab-style caftan beneath, the rabbits realized that this was no ordinary brain surgeon but one of the Fat One's close adjutants,. Whoever it was, he was furious and roared out a threat that he would get even with the rabbits for reducing his brain surgeons to tears. He then stormed out of the club before the rabbits had a chance to react.

In fact, the rabbits continued with their program as if nothing had happened, rolling down a huge movie screen and started showing the flagellation scene from "The Seventh Seal". Whips were distributed to the customers, including the brain surgeons, and all the animals and surgeons crawled around on their knees, singing "You cut me up!" and whipping themselves as they continued this strange nocturnal parade.

And at the center, perched atop a 20-gallon drum of carrot beer, arms folded, sat Commander Zeko, grinning ear to ear. Truly an evening to remember.

15

Cloud Riding

"Did you see us up there?" Zeko asked excitedly.

"Where?"

"On the clouds, up on the clouds. Did you see us up there?

"Huh?" Kris and I were not especially alert. After all, it was a lazy Sunday morning and we were not required to be alert.

Zeko raced on, scarcely noticing our limp reactions. "It was wonderful up there, and so comfortable, just sitting on the clouds. From down here they look like they are hardly moving, but in fact they are gliding steadily, but gently, like bubbles blown across an open veranda. It was so relaxing."

"Where's Sacher?" I asked, thinking that Sacher might be a more reliable source. But Sacher was nowhere around.

"It was just Sacher and me up there," Zeko continued.

"I'll bet!"

"It was like nothing else in life. And we dyed the clouds for you...."

No reaction from us.

"You mean you didn't notice?" Zeko asked. There was more than a hint of disappointment in her voice.

"No, sorry. I didn't notice anything," I admitted.

"I noticed," Kris helped out. "A beautiful pink."

"And yellow too," Zeko reminded her excitedly.

"That's right," Kris acknowledged. "Beautiful colors. But how did you do it? How does one go about dyeing clouds?"

"Oh, silly," said Zeko, "with cloud dye, of course. You should know that."

Just then Sacher walked in, with a big silly grin on her face.

"You look like you're as high as a kite," I said to Sacher.

"We *were*, up there in the clouds," Sacher replied. "Didn't Zeko tell you?"

"Weren't the birds a bit surprised to see two rabbits up there, cloud-riding?" Kris asked.

"I don't think so," Sacher replied. "Why should they be? After all, we weren't surprised to see *them* up there."

"That's right," said Zeko, giving unnecessary emphasis to this point. "We weren't surprised at all. Everything was just normal, very normal."

We didn't have a chance to reply to this last comment because there was suddenly a knock at the door. It was John and Vera.

"Hi guys!" said Vera in a joyful mood. "Hi rabbits!"

"Hi Vera," Zeko and Sacher said in unison. "What's new?"

"I just got my hair done," Vera replied. "Do you like it?"

"It's gorgeous, Vera," said Sacher gallantly.

"Thank you, Sacher," Vera replied.

"I can hear the rabbits!" John suddenly exclaimed in wild excitement. "I can hear them! They're talking!"

"Oh that's right, I hear them too," said Vera, suddenly realizing that she had been conversing with stuffed animals.

"I can hear them!" John repeated.

"You already said that," Zeko observed. "But if it's any consolation, we can hear you as well."

"This is incredible," said Vera. "What happened?"

"Maybe you got your hearing fixed," Sacher wisecracked.

"Oh, Sacher, be nice," I said, and then to John and Vera: "I think you are getting to know the rabbits. Sometimes you have to know someone for a while before you can hear that person properly."

"Hey, let's do 'stuffed animal' imitations," Zeko suggested, stiffening her limbs and tumbling off the arm of the armchair and landing on the cushion upside down.

"Watch me!" Sacher announced, freezing her limbs in straight lines, fixing her eyes in a glazed stare, and immediately toppling over and landing on a blanket and looking very stuffed indeed.

This looked like fun. So pretty soon we were all doing 'stuffed animal' imitations, lying around looking like we were waiting for children to come along and pick us up.

"Hey, are we allowed to talk like this!" Vera asked.

"Ssshhh!" said Zeko. "Stuffed animals aren't supposed to talk, and especially not when they are imitating stuffed animals!" We all giggled at this joke.

Actually, Zeko's last comment seemed to raise both semantic and philosophical questions, but none of us could be bothered to pursue them except that John suddenly announced, "I have a quote from Nietzsche!"

"OK, let's have it," I said.

"It was on the occasion of a surprise birthday party being

thrown for him on his 42nd birthday, and what he said was, 'Hey, everybody, let's get wild and crazy!'"

"And he practised what he preached, too," Sacher observed.

"No, this is a seriously crazy proposal I want to make," said John. "Let's all go to Otaru."

So it was that the six of us piled into John's car, without so much as reflecting on Nietzsche's other thoughts, and set out for Otaru, a town founded in the 1880s and renowned for its canals. No doubt drawing inspiration from its canals, Otaru began sometime in the 1950s to think of itself as a "little Venice" and began filling the town with Italian paraphernalia, including a Museo dell'Arte Veneziana, an enormous Italian marble clock, imported Italian gondolas, Italian restaurants, and lots and lots of Italian music. As we neared the town, we picked up Radio Otaru, which was playing Pavarotti most of the way. But as we reached the city limits, the program switched to the greatest hits of Nicola di Bari:

> *Amore, ritorna a casa,*
> *Prego, torna da me.*
> *Ho paura del mondo*
> *Senza di te.*
> *Amore, amore, amore.*

We all sang along. It was an old favorite.

Otaru looked much the way it does on the postcards, except that there was a strange magical glitter in the air that we could not account for. We parked the car and stood on the bridge, posing for photos and taking turns behind the lens.

Suddenly Sacher seemed to remember something. "Comrades!" she screamed, "we have a good friend here in Otaru. I almost forgot. We *must* look him up."

"Who?" we all said.

"Why, il Dottore Ottavio del Paese -- an old friend from our experimental science days," replied Sacher.

"Oh yes, Ottavio, what a sweet fellow," chimed in Zeko. "And brilliant too. You will never in your life meet someone as brilliant as il Dottore Ottavio del Paese."

"Hold on," said John. "This name sounds imaginary. Del Paese -- what kind of name is that?"

"He's from the country," Zeko explained.

"And he's Italian? Why is there an Italian living in Otaru?" John persisted.

"Come on," said Zeko, "you're not surprised to find Italian-style canals and an Italian-style museum in Otaru, or to hear Italian music here, or to be able to enjoy the best spaghetti alla bolognese this side of Bologna. But finding an Italian living here in this very Italian atmosphere strikes you as surprising!"

"No, no, of course not," said John, backing off.

"Where does he live?" Vera asked, offering the rabbits the necessary opening.

"We'll show you," they replied.

We walked the short distance. We had to go up a very small hill, turn at a white picket fence, and then continue along a small gravel path that seemed to get steadily narrower and more winding. And we noticed that the farther we walked, the more shrubs and trees there were. Finally, when the path was barely 10" wide, we reached a huge gate and went in. It was the zoo.

"OK, fess up," I said. "We're going to visit one of the animals, right? Dr. Ottavio del Paese is an animal."

"He's not a plant, if that's what you mean," said Zeko.

"Just be patient," Sacher advised. "Patience is prudence and prudence is joy but asking and pressing can only annoy." As usual, Sacher was right.

We didn't have to wait long. We bought our tickets; the rabbits, of course, got in free, no doubt due to their good connections in Otaru. We passed the lions and the tigers, the bears and the elephants, the winged octopi and the kerguelan horned vultures, and finally reached the chimpanzee cage. Sacher then went up to the cage and called in, "Dr. del Paese, some friends are here to visit."

Most of the chimpanzees in the cage were naked. So, I will confess, I was a little surprised when one of them, wearing a checkered jacket, cotton trousers, finely pressed white shirt, and a red flannel bowtie came up to us. The effect was completed with an English bowler hat, a hand-crafted cane, and a fine watch on a gold chain. "Hello Zeko and Sacher. It's been a long time," said this chimpanzee, and then, turning to us, he added, "Hello, friends. I am il Dottore Ottavio del Paese at your service."

We all introduced ourselves. Even John was very respectful.

"My abode is very humble," Dr. del Paese said, in what struck me as an unintended understatement. "But please take a chair."

"Take a chair?" Vera asked. "But there aren't any!"

"That's why I advise you to take along your own," Dr. del Paese replied. "Because I cannot offer you any. Can I offer you some tea?"

"Can you?" Kris asked, looking a little troubled.

"No, I'm sorry," Dr. del Paese apologized. "I seem to have lost my tea pot." I was starting to get the impression that Dr. del Paese had once lived in finer circumstances and had prided himself on etiquette and ritual; now, in leaner circumstances, he still had need to recall the rituals of yesteryear.

"That's OK," Kris replied through the bars of the cage. "We are fine like this."

"Dr. del Paese is the world expert on lizard droppings," Zeko declared, looking very proud to know such an important person. "He's been studying them for 22 years."

"Dr. del Paese is the world expert on lizard droppings," Zeko declared, looking very proud to know such an important person. "He's been studying them for 22 years."

"23 actually," Dr. del Paese corrected Zeko. "I have found that lizard droppings come in three basic shapes, elongated, compact, and runny, and that there is a rare strain of lizards high in the Andes mountains whose droppings are fluorescent. One of the most beautiful sights anywhere in the world is the multicolored glow of fluorescent lizard droppings in the Andes mountains. Sometime you have to see this."

"But why lizard droppings?" I asked. "What can you do with them?"

"This is a good question," Dr. del Paese answered. "It is, of course, the essential question, the question to which I have been devoting myself these many years. I have been developing ways of using lizard droppings to improve the quality of life."

"Yes, yes," said Zeko excitedly. "Dr. del Paese has developed a bath soap from lizard droppings."

"Imagine the pleasure of bathing in lizard droppings," said Sacher, smiling earnestly.

"I can hardly wait," said John.

"Where can we get some?" Vera wanted to know.

"Well, it's not on the market yet," Dr. del Paese admitted. "But I am also developing some other products from lizard droppings, including face cream and perfume. I call the face cream Reptile: Reptile Facial Cream. It sounds enticing, doesn't it?"

"What will you call the perfume?"

"I'm not sure yet," Dr. del Paese admitted. "But it has a wonderful scent. The flies just love it." He pulled out a small bottle and sprayed it in the air. We all instinctively drew back.

"Maybe you could call it Unexpected Use, since no one would have thought to use lizard droppings for a perfume," Kris suggested.

"Or how about Guess Again," John suggested.

"Too complicated," answered Dr. del Paese. "I think I just call it Lizard Dropping Perfume."

"Some of your research probably has military uses too, I would surmise," I said, perhaps a bit impertinently.

"From lizard droppings? Of course. The best poison gas war materiel comes from lizard droppings. Also jet fuel," Dr. del Paese noted with pride. But he must have been revealing trade secrets, because the rabbits looked at him very crossly, and he immediately changed the subject. "Lizard droppings also have musical uses, in symphonic concerts, for example. They can even be used as a cocoa substitute in chocolate."

"No, they cannot," said Zeko archly.

"Have you tried the substitution?" asked the good dottore.

"No, and we don't intend to," replied Zeko. "We have our own formulas for chocolate, and none of them involve lizard droppings."

"Do you do all your research alone," John asked the doctor, "or do you have collaborators?"

"Si, collaborators, I have collaborators," Dr. del Paese replied. "Many collaborators. But my most important collaborator is Professor Kotoba Waza, a most refined and elegant gentleman."

"Is he here in the cage with you?"

"No, unfortunately," Dr. del Paese replied. "The zoo-keepers are very primitive and insist on strict species segregation. Who ever heard of such a thing? I have tried over and over again to obtain at least an exemption for Professor Waza, but the answer is always the same: 'We're not going to put any pink flamingo in the chimpanzee cage.' So our collaboration is very difficult."

"Where can we find Professor Waza?" I asked.

Before Dr. del Paese could answer, however, Sacher offered, "Come, we'll take you to meet him."

So we bade farewell to il dottore Ottavio del Paese, the world expert on lizard droppings, and started down the path to the main pond. As we were walking, we suddenly heard a jubilant del Paese shouting excitedly behind us, "Ice cream! Yes, I can make lizard dropping ice cream! Incredible!"

The pond was not far, and we were able to pass through the bird sanctuary along the way, viewing many rare species of birds, including the blue-bearded warblers, the self-righteous furry bug-suckers, the bare-breasted table-peckers, the full-chested twig-snappers, and that rarest of all birds, the Andorran three-eyed water thrush. Finally, we reached the lily pond and there they were -- 16 absolutely gorgeous pink flamingoes, one of whom was certainly Professor Kotoba Waza. As usual, the flamingoes were resting on one leg; some of them were clearly asleep and were even snoring loudly. I had never heard pink flamingoes snore before. Fortunately several of them were awake. Indeed, they were rapt in conversation about Goethe's *Faust*. One of their number spied us, and nodded to us in greeting. Sizing us up through his monocle he addressed us collectively, "Hello, can I help you? Are you looking for anyone in particular? Or are you just tourists deriving some perverted thrill from gawking at members of other species?"

"No," Zeko answered. "We are not tourists. I am Commander Zeko. I am sure that you have heard of me. These are my friends. We are friends of Dr. del Paese and are eager to meet his collaborator, Professor Kotoba Waza."

"I am Professor Waza," said the flamingo with the monocle. "Ottavio del Paese is a dear friend, and any friends of his are friends of mine. Hop over the fence if you like. Perhaps you would like to rest a leg with us."

We declined his friendly offer and asked him about his work and interests.

"Ah," Professor Waza replied as if thinking deeply. "You are interested in my work. I am the inventor of Aromavision. Television that lets you smell what you see. Imagine the olfactory ecstasy you will experience as you watch, in sequence, a perfume commercial, a dog-food commercial, and a commercial for car tires. It will be truly splendid. It will be heavenly. It will be glorious. That is my crowning achievement so far."

As we conversed further with Professor Waza, it turns out that he and il Dottore del Paese had become involved in a whole series of money-making schemes, few of which made them any money. There was, for example, the indulgence-of-the-month club, granting members plenary indulgences for certain offenses on a month-by-month basis. The Holy See was not amused. But more to the point, there were very few takers. They were forced to shut down the club after just four months. Then there was their attempt at creating what they called Jazz Dental. "Jiving dentists fix your teeth to the latest hot jazz." The idea was that you go in, sit in the dentist's chair, and find your dentist dancing and jiving as he sticks his instruments into your mouth. That experiment was likewise a failure. Then they thought of a companion set to go along with *The Great Books of the Western World*. They called it *The Not-So-Great Books of the Western World*, figuring that people don't always want to read serious stuff. That may be, but *The Great Books* geared up for a law suit and they had to discontinue their line even before they had it on the market. Their latest joint venture was to establish an institute. They called it the Institute for Global Solutions.

"We need more global solutions," said John, seeming very impressed. "How is it organized?" John always had a good mind for organizational questions.

"We have several divisions. One of these divisions is the Division for Comprehensive Solutions," Professor Waza explained. "In addition to serving as co-director of the institute, I am also head of this division. But we have other divisions, such as the Division for Partial Solutions."

"That doesn't sound so promising," I mused aloud.

"It's not. Part of the problem is that its director is a parrot, and he just keeps repeating everything he hears, without even thinking about it. A real bird-brain. His division messes everything up. They are always leaving things out. Such silly people. We of the Division for Comprehensive Solutions understand that if you are going to get anywhere, you must first take everything into account. Otherwise, you just end up in a mess."

"So why do you keep them around?" I asked.

"It's part of our solution for unemployment. We at the Division for Comprehensive Solutions invented their division, in order to give them jobs and keep them off the lily pads. But they don't really contribute anything useful."

"One minute," Vera said. "Why would parrots want to sit on the lily pads?"

"I am so sorry," began Professor Waza. "I forgot to mention that only the director of this division is a parrot. All the other researchers in this division are frogs. Of course that means that the parrot sometimes runs around muttering 'ribit, ribit, ribit' as if he were a frog or something."

"What about other divisions?" asked Sacher.

"Yes, yes, of course," replied Professor Waza. "We have a third division. It is called the Division for Impossible Solutions. You see, when people think about solutions, they always want something that you can actually do. But this means that you always leave out some things. The Division for Impossible Solutions was established to address this deficiency. Last year, for example, this division solved the problems of global overpopulation and environmental damage."

"What did they propose? What did they say?" Vera asked impatiently.

"Oh, fine things," answered Professor Waza. "Send large numbers of people to Mars, erect a giant fan to blow the pollution off the planet, and rearrange the chemical composition of desert sand to turn it into chewy candy. That division is our most energetic division, and even puts out a magazine: *Impossible Solutions for Everyday Life*. Do you want to subscribe?"

The rabbits declined, noting that they were busy with their Café. But the rest of us eagerly took out subscriptions. I could hardly wait to see my first copy, I thought to myself as I paid Professor Waza for the subscription.

By this point, all of us were getting very excited about going to the Museo dell'Arte Veneziana -- that is, all of us except John, who insisted that he would not be caught dead "in such a place." I wonder what he meant by that. But the vote was 5 to 1; and now we literally marched to the Museo (Zeko calling cadence). Vera, Kris, and I, together with the two rabbits, went in. John stayed outside, stuffing an enormous wad of tobacco into his pipe. Then, setting it ablaze, he stuffed the pipe into his mouth, so that he could enjoy this small bonfire close to his face.

Vera, Kris, and I bought our entry tickets. As usual, the rabbits got in free. (How do they do it?) We entered into the main hall, in the center of which was a long pool of water, with a rather meretriciously decorated and oversized gondola sitting in the middle of it. On one side of the gondola were several shops -- one selling local glass figurines, another selling postcards of Venice and Italian calendars, and a third shop offering Italian silk scarves and pantomime masks. The other side of the gondola was dominated by a wide rococo staircase framed by a marble arch. To the left of the staircase there was a wine merchant, displaying fine wines from northern Italy. And to the right, there was a string octet, attired in fashions from the Italian baroque period, and playing Vivaldi's "Four Seasons." Around the hall and along the staircase were a number of masked mannequins.

Zeko and Sacher pulled us toward the arch, and as we passed through it, something quite marvelous happened: Vivaldi's "Four Seasons" dissolved into Debussy's "Nuages", and the masked mannequins, which had looked inanimate to us a moment before, drew around us, parting in front of us, pulling back, and beckoning us upward. The air seemed to sparkle.

Then it happened. Reality slowed down, and formless vapors sifted into our minds, conjuring a perplexing array of disconnected images that left us disoriented. We asked for a museum brochure. The museum curator offered us our choice of Russian, German, Italian, English, and Japanese versions. We took one of each. Best to be on the safe side. Maybe there are some differences from one to the other. We'll need to check into this, Kris thought to herself. Copies of 15th-century Italian paintings. Copies of 16th-century Italian paintings. Copies of 17th-century Italian paintings. Copies of authentic furniture of the period. Copies of authentic masterpieces of Italian sculpture of the late renaissance. Copies of authentic gondolas designed by the Italian master, Persipio da Udine.

John missed all this, of course, and when we eventually emerged into the daylight, he was very intently stuffing a new pack of tobacco into his pipe. "So how was the museum?" he asked.

"It was very interesting," Sacher assured him. "We liked it."

John took another huge wad of tobacco and tried to stuff it into his already full pipe. He struck a match, scarcely noticing that his pipe was over-stuffed, and ignited it.

"John," I said, "that is the most peculiar-smelling tobacco I have ever had the displeasure to smell. Where did you get it?"

"It's a gift from il Dottore Ottavio del Paese," he told us.

"Let me see the package," said Vera, taking it into her hands. "John, I think you're smoking lizard droppings!" We all giggled at his.

"Well, that accounts for the distinctive taste," John commented, continuing to puff happily on his pipe.

It had been a wonderful day. A day to remember. And as we drove home again, singing Neapolitan songs and exchanging reminiscences about Italy, Sacher suddenly turned to Zeko and whispered in her ear. Apparently they had some important business to attend to.

16

A Trip to Planet Xypon

I suddenly became aware that there was a tremendous amount of clattering, banging, sliding, and miscellaneous other noises, including regular clanging thuds of metal against metal. "Kris," I raised my voice to make myself heard, "what is all that noise?"

"It's the rabbits," she explained matter-of-factly.

"I figured that, but where are they and what are they doing?"

"They are in the basement, building a spaceship," Kris answered.

"We don't have a basement," I objected.

"Well, that's where they are." Kris seemed satisfied with this answer.

"How can they be in the basement if we don't have a basement in this building?" I persisted.

"Do you want to know where the rabbits are, or do you want to discuss the layout of this building?" That settled things as far as Kris was concerned.

"OK," I said, giving in. "I want to know where the rabbits are. So where are they?"

"They are in the basement, Bill."

"Hrumpf," I mumbled in exasperation.

Kris continued with her work, but after a few moments, I returned to the theme: "They are building a *what?!?*"

"A spaceship."

"Oh good -- so now they're going to fly to Mars maybe."

"Why don't you ask them where they are going, if you want to know?"

"Because they are in the basement which doesn't exist," I replied cleverly. "Maybe our magical rabbits can go to places which don't exist, but I can't."

"Well, it's good practice for you to admit your limitations," Kris replied.

"You're beginning to sound like the rabbits," I said.

Just then Sacher walked in, looking rather tired and wiping the perspiration from her brow. "I'd like a lemonade," Sacher indicated, as if addressing one of Café Bombshell's waitresses. She turned on the television, just in time for a commercial:

Two adolescent boys are strolling happily through the woods.
Rod: "Say, Gus, what kind of brain paste do you use?"
Gus: "Why I use Crano-Glow. It gives me a fresh and vivacious feeling and leaves my brain shiny and feeling tingly all over."
Rod: "Gee, I wish I had a shiny brain. But all my brushing only succeeds in making me drowsy."
Gus: "Crano-glow will give you zip, wake you up. It

contains a patented ingredient called Alertadent which annihilates drowsiness on contact. Alertadent bubbles and fizzes the accumulated mucous, and vaporizes mildew and other organic residues. Try Crano-Glow. You won't be disappointed."

Rod: "I *will*. It sounds like just the thing."

"There, did you see that?" I said in triumph, pointing to the television.

"Sure," agreed Sacher. At last I had a definite witness. "It's just another commercial for brain paste. The brain surgeons are behind it. It's an international conspiracy. Now where's my lemonade?"

"I'll get you a lemonade," I offered, "but perhaps you would be so good as to tell us what is going on downstairs, or wherever your 'basement' is."

"Basements are always downstairs," Sacher explained in a kindly voice. "The location is part of the definition of the word. If the basement were upstairs, it wouldn't be a basement at all; it would be an attic. So of course it's downstairs."

"But we don't *have* a downstairs!" I sighed, hopelessly, sliding the lemonade glass across the counter toward Sacher.

"Comrade, you are getting all upset over things that don't concern you. We're doing all the work. We don't ask you to come downstairs to help. So why do you get so ruffled?" Sacher was the very picture of reason tempered by prudence.

"Where are you going in your spaceship?" I asked, switching gears.

Sacher was slurping her lemonade noisily. But after a few hefty gulps and a very contented burp, Sacher smiled and told us: "We're going to Xypon."

"Xypon?" we both stuttered, in confusion.

"Planet Xypon, in the constellation Argos. It's about 283,000,000,000,000 light years from here. I'll read to you from the travel brochure," Sacher offered, pulling a small brochure out of her pocket. She started to read, in an especially wiry voice: "Next time you are in the constellation Argos, be sure to visit Planet Xypon. Xyponese are renowned throughout the constellation for their hospitality, their charm, and their tendency to glow in the dark. Visit the exotic slime pits of Xypon's poles. Sample the bark of Xypon's incredible choco-late-covered petrified bubbles (they're very tasty). Take a fer-ry cruise across Xypon's vast lava oceans and marvel at the unique behavior of Xypon's magnetic volcanic ash.

"The equatorial stretches of Planet Xypon," Sacher contin-ued reading, "consist of hot turbid flows of lava which ooze out from the porous surface beneath. Local inhabitants spend most of their lives on metal-fitted boats which sail on the lava. The two-ringed planet also has two suns, and as one sets on one side of the horizon, the other rises on the other side -- "

"Let me see that brochure," I interrupted.

"Private property," Sacher replied, and stuffed the bro-chure back into her pocket. "Time to get back to work."

"Yes, mustn't keep Zeko waiting."

The banging and clanging and wanging and zanging con-tinued the rest of the day and into the night. It was a Monday night, so Café Bombshell was closed, and the noise contin-ued until about 3:30 a.m. Kris and I were amazed that none of our neighbors complained about all the noise. Perhaps they were all deaf. Or all working night shifts. Finally, the rabbits stopped work, came back to bed, and fell asleep. Come sweet slumber.

The next thing I was aware of was Zeko's voice, coming over a loudspeaker, beginning a countdown. "10...9...8..." Kris and I flew out of bed and dashed out to the living room. "...7...6..." There it was, in the middle of our living room: a small rocket ship, perhaps 20 feet in length, pointing toward the window. "...5...4...3..." The sliding glass door facing the balcony was open and the screen fixtures had been removed. "Where are the rabbits?" "...2...1..." "They must be on board!" "Oh, no!" "...Zero...Blast-off!"

Spplurrrggh ploooooff! The rocket ship spewed out a tremendous cloud of indigo blue smoke that smelled like the best French perfume, and gazooks!, the spaceship lifted off the ground and slowly floated out the window. It wasn't going to make it to Planet Xypon anytime soon, not at that speed, we thought to ourselves. It continued to spew out sweetly scented blue smoke. Then, after about 20 seconds of gently floating forwards, the spaceship abruptly switched to a supersonic velocity and in a flash -- Pfloom!! -- it was no more to be seen -- leaving only a well-defined blue trail behind.

They were gone four or five days, and, frankly, we missed them. Their return was, however, not nearly as majestic as their departure. What happened is that Kris and I were straightening up the apartment and, as Kris adjusted the cushion on one of the armchairs, she saw the rabbits curled up underneath, fast asleep.

"Hey, what are you guys doing here?" she asked in considerable surprise.

"I thought you guys were on Xypon!" I blurted out.

"We're sleeping," Zeko declared in her usual imperious tone of voice.

"We're sleeping," Sacher repeated, semi-consciously, sounding completely bleary-eyed. "We're exhausted..." Sacher started to nod off again.

"We're busy!" Zeko said as if it were an ultimatum -- her favorite phrase again.

"Maybe you guys never made it to Xypon, huh?" I suggested.

"So, did you get to Xypon?" Kris asked, a bit more delicately than I.

"OK, OK, I give up," said Zeko in a tone that suggested anything but surrender. "You win. We don't get any sleep. You want information. We went to Xypon. It's covered with hot lava oceans, freezing slime pits, and vast expansive fields of petrified bubbles, just like the travel brochure says. Now may we go back to sleep?" And Zeko collapsed back into the chair with such force that Sacher rolled off the chair and fell onto the floor. Zeko didn't even notice and was soon snoring very loudly, even -- or so it sounded to me -- aggressively.

Sacher sat upright on the floor and massaged her head a little; after a few moments, she turned to us, flashed us one of her winning smiles, and asked, "Do you want to hear about Planet Xypon?"

"Yes, yes, we do," we said in unison. And Sacher began: "It's a smallish planet, maybe half the size of earth, but its suns are even smaller, so that the two suns rotate around Xypon, rather than the other way around. So you couldn't call it a solar system. We landed during the day there, which was convenient -- of course, we couldn't land during the night anyway, because with two rotating suns, Planet Xypon never has night, only endless day.

"We landed on one of their steel-fitted boats. At first we didn't see anyone, only what looked to us like long rows of six-branched trees. We walked a bit, not saying anything, looking for some sign of life. Finally, Zeko muttered something to me, and all at once one of these trees greeted us in a very friendly tone of voice, and in fluent English. The voice came out from one of these branches. I decided to see if they knew any Arabic, and so I spoke to the same tree which had addressed us, but this time in Arabic, and again I received a fluent and very friendly reply, only this time from a different branch. Zeko tried out her Italian and a third branch turned out to know Italian. We then started to converse with this tree in Italian and it turned out that these trees were the most intelligent life on Planet Xypon, the rulers of the planet. As we continued to talk to this tree, a couple of other trees joined us and joined in the conversation. They were all very friendly, asked about our trip, did we need to rest, and insisted on serving us a fine meal produced from local Xyponese shrubs. They even had a local vegetable that looked something like a carrot, only it was flaming pink and gave off a bright glow. It tasted excellent, very sweet, but had the effect of making us want to turn somersaults. The trees were eating these pink carrots too and pretty soon all of us were turning somersaults and giggling like crazy.

"We found out many things about their society. For example, only six languages are spoken on all of Xypon, and everyone speaks all of these languages. The tree-creatures divide up the talent in a rather unique way, with each branch fluent in a different language. When we heard this, we were very impressed. I turned to Zeko and said, 'They must have some excellent language instructors here,' and the trees all smiled and hummed with contented pride. Their six languages are English, German, Italian, Arabic, Xyponese, and Teronese."

"What is Teronese?" Kris and I asked.

"Teronese is the indigenous language of the Planet Teron, which is only 110 light-years distant from Xypon. They're neighbors, so to speak. But they seem to have troubled relations."

"What kind of government do they have?"

"This was hard for us to determine. As far as we could tell, decisions are taken by a rustling of leaves and humming at different pitches, dispensing with polemics. Maybe it's some sort of democracy."

Zeko was awake. "What I liked best on Planet Xypon was finding out that Marlene Dietrich is on their 10-lava bill," said Zeko. "We asked about that, and they said they all know and love the music of Marlene Dietrich. They told us that 'Lili Marlene' is their planetary anthem."

"Also," Sacher resumed the narrative, "Xypon is a no-smoking planet. There is no tobacco-smoking allowed anywhere on the planet; there are not even any smoking areas."

"Do they grow tobacco at all?" I asked, since if there was no tobacco, then it could not help but be a no-smoking planet.

"Oh yes, plenty of it," Sacher answered.

"It's used in the penal system," Zeko explained with a sly grin spreading across her lips. "If anyone commits a crime, this person is locked up for life in a penal colony inside the largest slime pit on the planet. There the inmates are supplied with all the cigarettes they could possibly want."

"OK, what if they don't smoke?" Kris asked.

"Tobacco is also burned 24 hours a day in large prison ovens, and the fumes are pumped in through the air-conditioning system. So everyone smokes in prison -- with or without cigarettes."

"Sounds awful," I commented.

"Oh, I'm sure it *is* awful," Sacher agreed, smiling warmly, as if we were talking about something very pleasant.

"They probably all get lung cancer and emphysema..."

"They have their own diseases," Zeko noted, "which are a bit different. After all, have you ever seen a tree with lung cancer? But it comes down to much the same thing."

"So what were you two doing on Xypon anyway -- just a little innocent tourism?" I asked. "Or did your trip have maybe something to do with fighting the brain surgeons?"

"So many questions," Zeko noted. "Sacher, doesn't Bill have a lot of good questions?"

"Yes," Sacher agreed, smiling amiably, "lots of good questions."

"You have a very inquisitive mind," Zeko said. "Bright fellow. Yes, very bright."

"That's why we like you."

"Because you're so bright."

"It reminds me of the time -- "

"So you're not going to tell me, eh?" I pressed.

"Tourism!" Zeko replied evasively. "We went there because we wanted to look around and have a pleasant time."

"That sounds pretty unlikely to me," I replied.

But just then, Kris cut the conversation short. "My gosh, you two must be exhausted after your big trip," Kris said.

"Thanks for noticing," said Zeko dryly.

"How was the trip back?"

"Oh, fine," said Sacher. "It was very fine."

"So where's the spaceship?" I asked.

"It's back in the basement, of course," replied Zeko. "Where else?"

"Of course. At least we won't have to worry about cleaning up."

17

Robotized Weasels

"What are we going to do with those weasels?" Sacher muttered, half to herself, as she tapped her fingers on the kitchen table. "What are we going to do?" Kris and I were preparing our breakfast. The rabbits, as usual, had it easy, and were being waited on.

"They hardly talk any more," Zeko elucidated. "Lobotomized, totally lobotomized. It's all good and fine that the brain surgeons have stopped lobotomizing our customers, but these weasels are in dreadful shape. And besides, this may be just a temporary respite. Who knows when the brain surgeons will resume lobotomizing innocent creatures."

"They are really a pitiful sight," Sacher added, just in case we had missed the point.

"What about brain transplants?" I suggested. "Surely you can find some suitable donors."

"You mean from some dying animal?"

"Yes, sure. Something like that."

"So we just wait for some weasel, with a functioning brain, to get into serious physical condition and then make a swap. Sounds like a full-body transplant to me, not a brain transplant," Sacher objected. "And besides, we don't hear about many cases of mangled weasels needing new bodies."

"What about from a duck or something," Kris suggested. "Ducks are always getting into trouble, aren't they?"

"Yeah," Zeko answered, "but can you imagine a duck brain in a weasel body! I can just imagine the thing trying to socialize with 'other' ducks! Or trying to quack!"

"I have an idea," Kris looked inspired. "What about artificial intelligence?! Install a small computer in their heads, or even a big computer."

"Hmmn," the rabbits said in unison. "Hmmn."

"It's worth thinking about."

"It just might work."

"I wonder..."

The rabbits discussed the idea with their staff of physicists, geneticists, computer programmers, and specialists in artificial intelligence, a staff which made Café Bombshell the envy of every other café in town. With such impressive talent on board, they eventually came up with a solution. What they did sounds, in retrospect, perfectly obvious. First, they installed a highly sophisticated computer in each of these weasel's heads -- each with a memory capacity of 24,000,000,000 megabytes. They spent about two months installing programs. A program for basic vocabulary and sound recognition, with fluency in English, Japanese, German, and Italian. A program for responding to questions about food in any of these languages. A program for responding to questions about the time, the weather, and about one's health. A program loaded with information about ancient Greek and Renaissance philosophy. A program with elaborate and detailed information about classical music from Palestrina to Philip Glass. A program with detailed knowledge about and 'opinions' about various classics of American, English, Japanese, Russian, German, and Italian literature. A program equipping them with rudimentary information about world history from the time of Homer. A program with information about the plot lines of such classic films as *The Cowboy from Brooklyn* (1938), *An Angel from Texas* (1940), *Bedtime for Bonzo* (1951), *Cattle Queen of Montana* (1954), and *Tennessee's Partner* (1955). A program enabling the intelligence unit to combine concepts, to assimilate and retain new information. A program for species recognition. A program with information about the feeding habits of various species.

The second step was a bit more subtle (though no less obvious,...in retrospect). Taking a small cell culture from each of these weasels, the scientific staff at Café Bombshell isolated each weasel's DNA, and separating out those parts relating to personality, created a cybernetic replication of each weasel's original personality in the form of a small "personality implant", which was surgically installed behind the left ear.

Since the weasels had almost without exception lost their previous jobs, the rabbits also graciously offered them jobs as waiters and waitresses at Café Bombshell. The entire operation was, evidently, a huge success. The rabbits were so pleased that they brought us bottles of champagne to celebrate. There were, in turns out, just two chinks in the program. The first was that the weasels tended to walk and move in jerky, rather mechanical ways, a bit reminiscent of old-fashioned robots. The second was that, because of a flaw in one of the programs -- caught only when it was too late -- the weasels began every reply with the statement, "Hello, I'm a weasel." The rabbits told us that with time, they hoped to work out this second chink. But in the meantime, it gave rise to some strange exchanges.

For example, one night a tiger showed up at the Club (Café Bombshell did not get many tigers as customers). The tiger took a table by himself, and of course, one of the friendly weasel-waiters was soon attending to his needs.

"Hello, I'm a weasel. I'm your waiter. Here is a copy of today's menu. Our special today is chateau broccoli with sauce bernaise and asparagus spears."

"Grrrooorr! What's the soup?" the tiger asked in a rough voice.

"Hello, I'm a weasel. Today's soup, back by popular demand, is cream of carrot soup."

In fact, on that particular night, about half of the customers in the club were rabbits, and almost all of them were enjoying this carrot soup.

"I can see you're a weasel," the tiger growled in a kind of snort. "I don't want carrot soup. Who's ever heard of a tiger eating carrot soup and broccoli? I want some meat. Raw meat. Where's steak tartare? I don't see it on your menu."

"Hello, I'm a weasel. I'm sorry, sir, we are a vegetarian restaurant. Our customers include all species and none of them would like to see their Aunt Mabel or Uncle Marvin on the dinner plate. As Spinoza once said -- "

"Shut up. I don't want to hear about Spinoza. I want meat. I'm a carnivore!"

"Hello, I'm a weasel -- "

"What are you, an idiot? Why do you keep repeating this line?"

"Hello, I'm a weasel. Your suggestion that I might be an idiot has no basis in fact. Actually, my artificially installed cranial capacity is approximately 120 times that of the average tiger." Maybe the Club's scientists should have installed a program for tact. At any rate, the tiger did not like this reply.

"Grrrooorr! Grrrooorr! Grrrooorr!" the tiger kept repeating, as if he was suffering from tourette syndrome. Or perhaps rage simply rendered him completely inarticulate. The tiger got up and just kept repeating the same thing over and over again. This was one of those occasions when the rabbits congratulated themselves on having hired a team of rhinos as bouncers for the Club. So two of those big rhinos came up to the tiger and asked him gently, "Good evening, sir, is anything the matter?"

The tiger immediately adopted the most jovial and charming disposition. "Why no, of course not," the tiger replied. "I was just standing up to get a better view of your fine Café. My, this is a lovely place. And I understand that you are serving broccoli with asparatus spears tonight. It's my favorite. And carrot soup. I just *love* carrot soup. It's my favorite." The tiger sat down, trying to look very sweet and innocent, but looking more like a chastened little boy.

In a Club with a staff like this -- specialized scientists, artificially brilliant weasel-waiters, and rhino-bouncers -- what could ever go wrong? The Club even had its own private firefighting squad. Elephants, of course.

When Kris heard this story, she objected, Why didn't the tiger just go over and eat the rabbits at the other tables.

"Oh come now," Sacher said sagely. "Have you ever been in a restaurant and seen one of the customers try to eat some of the other customers? Patrons of restaurants generally know how to behave in restaurants. They have at least a rough idea that they order their food from a menu and that it is brought to them by waiters. Of course, maybe you are thinking of a self-service restaurant."

"Yes," Kris replied eagerly. "I was thinking of a self-service restaurant."

"Well," Zeko said with an air of finality, "Café Bombshell is not a self-service restaurant. And frankly, the whole idea sounds pretty dangerous to me!"

But, to get back to the weasels, they soon created complications of a new order. After six attempts to schedule the famous troupe of whistling alligators, the rabbits succeeded in

The whistling alligators offered a wide range of popular favorites, including "Swanee River".

bringing them in. The alligators dazzled the audience with virtuoso renditions of "Stars and Stripes Forever", "Wien, Stadt meiner Träume", "Celito Lindo", "La Cumparsita", and "Way Down Upon the Swanee River," among others. When they started in on "Lili Marlene", the rabbits wondered, maybe the alligators had also been to Xypon (?). Perhaps they had even done a whistling tour of Xypon. Perhaps that was why they had been so hard to book. Sometimes when it is hard to get together with other people (including alligators), it's because they are temporarily on other planets: that's a good rule of thumb to keep in mind.

At any rate, as the alligators launched into their final number, an amazing polyphonic display fashioned around best-loved tunes by Gabrieli, those irrepressible weasels suddenly joined in, displaying every bit as much brilliance and artistry as the alligators. The patrons were shocked.

"Evidently, the learning program installed in their cranial units is truly remarkable," Sacher conceded, "but unfortunately, our team of scientists forgot to install a program for common sense and good behavior. What are we going to do about those weasels?" And with that, Sacher started drumming her fingers on the kitchen table once again.

18

The International Brain Surgery Conspiracy

While Zeko and Sacher were busy running their night club and pretending to be filing reports on us, I had begun to probe into the activities of Sapporo's brain surgeons. Of course you can't be a very good detective if you don't know the local language. So I took a two-week crash course in Japanese, and learned enough to get by, and to recognize most of the kanji. Once you realize they're just pictograms, it's really very easy.

Armed with my new knowledge of Japanese and feeling confident of my abilities as an amateur sleuth, I began my investigations by combing the city, street by street, taking notes on the location and size of all brain surgery clinics. I had learned the benefits of keeping "complete records" from the rabbits. They always talk of the importance of keeping "complete records." When I had completed my preliminary research, I was amazed. Sapporo, a city with about one and a half million inhabitants, had 187 brain surgery clinics -- one for every 8,000 inhabitants. In fact, I found more brain surgery clinics in Sapporo than temples. And brain surgery isn't even a new religion. Or at least I don't think it is.

I needed to digest the facts I had collected. There is nothing like the music of Richard Wagner to help one to concentrate. So I put on my recording of Wilhelm Furtwaengler conducting the Vienna Philharmonic in Wagner's "Ride of the Valkyries" -- the 1949 recording -- full blast. At once my brain cells became activated. It was not long before I had formulated a plan of action.

I told Kris about my preliminary findings and my plan while she was baking cookies. She seemed to be concentrating very intently on the cookies, weighing each pat of dough before placing it on the cookie pan, and carefully placing exactly seven chocolate chips in each pat, always in the same array. She stared at her work with concentrated rapture as she continued with these procedures, all the while smiling to herself with self-evident satisfaction. But as for my findings, all she would say is, "That's nice Bill darling. That's *so* interesting." What's going on around here?, I thought to myself.

The rabbits did not display such equanimity, however, and warned me that the surgeons were dangerous people. They were not fine upstanding citizens like eco-terrorists or history professors. No, brain surgeons were a menace to society, just like polluters. So they told me, and I had no doubt about it. Since Kris was ignoring me, I told the rabbits of my plan to penetrate Sapporo's largest brain surgery clinic, the so-called Minnetaka Medical Facility for Brain Disorders. I invited them to come along, but the rabbits declined. It was "Cowboy Night" at Café Bombshell, and they were putting on a new act that night: the Faure Requiem rearranged as a hoe down. They expected a big crowd. OK, I said to myself, I'll go alone.

Kris scarcely noticed me leaving. By this point, with the latest batch of cookies in the oven, she was rearranging the ceramic figures on the kitchen shelf, carefully aligning them with the grains in the wood and placing them precisely 16 millimeters apart. She was even measuring the distance with a small ruler. She was busy. Nor did Astrolabe or Sexy take much cognizance of my presence; they were sprawled out on the kitchen floor that I had cleaned earlier that day, delighting in the aroma of freshly baked cookies. So I slipped out unnoticed, banging the door behind myself in the hope of possibly stirring her.

The Minnetaka Medical Facility was a long way from home, and I didn't have access to the rabbits' submarine. I had considered using public transport, but decided against this, in case I wanted to make a fast escape. So I donned my roller skates and skated to the facility. The Minnetaka Medical Facility had been built into an ancient Samurai Castle, dating from the fifteenth century, and was originally located on Honshu, south of Kyoto. But the fortress had been relocated to the hills overlooking Sapporo back in 1956, and from there one had a commanding view of the entire city. The fortress had been redesigned and refitted, up to a point, but it still retained much of its original appearance, including spiked iron gates at every entrance, each with a sliding portcullis that could be lowered by a turn of the crank, and stone turrets with narrow machicolations through which an archer might fire an arrow or dispatch some other projectile. As one crossed into the middle bailey, one could see a jolly little florist shop built into the barbican and what appeared to be a small food center built into what had originally been the tenshu (or keep). The overall effect was such as to give the impression of being a cross between a Samurai Castle and a health food store.

The Minnetaka Medical Facility had been built into an ancient Samurai Castle, dating from the fifteenth century.

I did not want to simply skate in through the main entrance. So I entered into the florist's shop, pretending to be interested in purchasing a bouquet. Every other Japanese florist I had ever seen had offered a very rich variety of flowers, but this florist had only one kind of flower: proteas. After comparing the offerings for a while, I pretended not to have found what I wanted, and slipped through the other door and entered into the main ward. I stole a blue gown, put it on quickly, and continued skating down a long corridor to the elevator. I knew from long experience, that the planning offices are always located on the top floor. So I pressed the button for the sixth floor, and began to glide upwards, my head feeling light with excitement. It seemed to me that I was seeing fluorescent bubbles floating about inside the elevator.

When we passed the fifth floor, the elevator light went out, and it was clear that the entire floor was unlit. Who knows what evil deeds were being perpetrated there! Perhaps that was the dungeon! But the lights came on a moment later, as I reached the sixth floor.

It would have been easy to have become distracted admiring all of the various artistic renderings of the human brain, by Matisse, Monet, Tintoretto, Titian, Rembrandt, Renoir, van Gogh, and many others. But I had to stick to business. I made my way to the Main Planning Room, sneaked inside and hid behind the coffee table, and listened carefully, taking out my notebook.

The brain surgeons were tap-dancing and singing this song in English:

If you're feeling moody or depressed,
No motivation to get yourself dressed,
We can forever erase that frown,
There's no need for you to feel down.
All we do is to cut inside
We guarantee you'll be satisfied
There's no need to be concerned,
None of our patients ever get burned.
We're brain surgeons, brain surgeons,
We've got our scalpels and blue gowns
We're brain surgeons, brain surgeons,
We can banish tears and frowns.

We just modify and fix your brain –
You won't remember the slightest pain –
You'll be singing a happy song,
No matter what disasters come along.
If your mood is slowing sinking
Maybe it's because you're thinking.

We can fix that problem once and for all,
You'll find our clinic at the shoppers' mall.
We're brain surgeons, brain surgeons,
Our medical knowledge is truly large
We're brain surgeons, brain surgeons,
We are meant to be in charge.

As they ended the song, they let out a big cheer, and then started to talk in Japanese. Unfortunately, my Japanese turned out not to be all that good, and I could not be entirely sure what they were saying, but from the few bits I *did* understand, and relying also on their body language, I have reconstructed the following exchange:

Dr. Watanabe: Our program of replacing natural brains with simulated brain implants is behind schedule. After eight months' of operations, we have only carried out 9,233 brain implants, and most of these were on weasels. And some of these operations have even been reversed by our sworn enemies, the two smart-alec rabbits who run Café Bombshell. If we are going to take over Sapporo, and from there, the Universe, we have to step up operations. We have orders from the Fat One, and he is getting impatient. Dr. Kraus-san, you are head of operations. What do you have to say for yourself?
Dr. Kraus: Sensai Watanabe-san, I am so sorry. It is entirely my fault. Please accept my most humble apologies. But staff is busy. Brain surgery is not so simple as changing a tire, it takes time, even when all you want to do is remove the natural brain and implant a suitable replacement. My assistant, Dr. Hidargo, and I have been working day and night to accelerate the pace of brain surgeries. Our kidnapping staff has done fine work, and we have also tried to attract volunteers

by plastering big posters on billboards all over the city. We have even sent 'salesmen' door-to-door, to offer free sample demonstrations to willing clients, but even on a 'no obligation' basis, we don't have so many takers. Except among the weasels."

Dr. Watanabe: "Well, this is unacceptable. Dr. Hidargo-san, we recruited you from the Madrid Medical Facility for Brain Implants. You are considered Spain's finest brain surgeon. But your results here are appalling. What do you have to say for yourself?"

Dr. Hidargo: "I am so sorry, Sensai Dr. Watanabe-san. We shall design a new demonstration for the door-to-door salesmen, and make bigger efforts with kidnapping. The implants are very good. The kidnapping must also be raised to the same high level. Long live the Minnetaka Medical Facility for Brain Disorders!"

This sounded like a toast, but among the 16 high-ranking surgeons seated around the table, not one had a drinking vessel of any kind. But it was then that one of them spied me, and sounded the alarm. I made for the door, and skated down the corridor, aware that there were 16 surgeons in blue gowns chasing after me. I made it to the elevator, the door closed, and I pressed the basement button. But to my dismay, the elevator stopped at the mysterious fifth floor, and I found the 16 men in blue gowns waiting for me there. They grabbed me, and hauled me off to a small padded cell, confiscating my skates. "You are crazy," one of them said to me in Japanese as they threw me into the cell. "You need brain surgery." I just know that's what he said.

19

Prisoner

They strapped me down on the bed, pulled a prison-grey blanket over me up to my neck, dimmed the lights, and turned on a television set. They left the room, thereupon, leaving me alone, unable to change the channel and condemned to watch the special Brain Surgery In-House television channel. Much of the fare was commercials. In fact, as I lay there, helpless, a commercial started up:

A slight man with a bandaged head, spectacles, and overalls is standing on a box in front of a gas station.

Bruno: "There are many gas stations for you to choose from, but there is only one gas station that also offers you instant brain implants while your gas is being pumped -- Crano-gas. You'll enjoy a wide selection of implants, providing you with detailed knowledge about Nathaniel Hawthorne, Hannibal Hamlin, the history of Tetovo, bridge construction and reconstruction, sea-faring, tap-dancing, yodeling, and many many more. We'll fill your head with facts and information and happy tunes. We'll fill your life. So when you drive into your local Crano-gas station and tell us 'Fill 'er up,' don't be surprised when we ask, 'The gas tank, the brain, or both?' And for a limited time only, we'll give you a free brain implant with every six-gallon purchase of gas."

That was a dismaying introduction. But then came the program: a light romance about a couple of happy young and beautiful brain surgeons who fall in love and go on picnics together amid the crocuses and the allysum and are just minding their own business until a couple of mean-spirited submarine commanders decide to spoil their fun and pour carrot juice all over their picnic spread. The so-called soundtrack consisted of the same four notes repeated indefinitely, without variation or modulation. The soundtrack was enough to drive me crazy and I'm sure it had some subliminal messages, even if I could not decipher them, and then there was that perverse disinformation about brain surgeons and submarine commanders to reckon with. There's nothing like bad propaganda to drive a person crazy. Give me good propaganda any day, something I can believe, or pretend to believe, but not this aggravating rubbish. I don't remember how long this dreary drivel droned on, driving me into a state of drastic dread, but eventually I fell asleep, dreaming about a patrol of drably dressed dragoons dragging away some drongo.

20

The Rescue

I woke up to see two blue-gowned surgeons staring at me pleasantly: an 85-year-old man with wavy black hair who bore an uncanny resemblance to some star in old B westerns, and a lady, who could scarcely have been much his junior, and who bore an uncanny resemblance to *him*.

"Hello," said the gentleman, caressing a scalpel he had brought with him. "I hope that you enjoyed our television entertainment. My name is Dr. Nero L. Granada. I shall be your operating physician. And this is Dr. Glenda Narone, who will assist me in the operation. We will remove the entire frontal lobe of your brain and replace it with a plastic bag, together with a small implant that will contain all the instructions that you will require."

"I won't sign the consent form and waiver," I pointed out obstreperously.

"We don't need that," Dr. Granada replied, continuing to smile warmly. "That would only be necessary in the event that you might file a complaint after the operation. That is, however, rather unlikely." He continued to smile. All of this seemed to be very pleasant for him. Dr. Narone also smiled in a friendly way. They obviously liked their work.

"Maybe you would like me to explain the sources of the Soviet-Yugoslav rift in 1948," I offered, confident of my ability to turn this into a *very* long story.

"No, we'll pass," said Dr. Narone. "We've read *Sheherazade*."

"How about an explanation of the life and times of Enver Hoxha?"

"No, we pass."

"How about the workings of Yugoslav self-management and the role of the self-managing interest communities?"

But they were ignoring me and wheeled me down the hall and into an operating room, where there were about eight or so other persons already assembled, as well as a lot of balloons and a long banner that read, "Hail to the volunteer!"

"You just lie here," said Dr. Granada, as if I had any other choice.

Click.

"The entire procedure will be over before you know it."

Click..., click.

"We'll just administer this anaesthesia and get started."

Click..., click..., ka-booooooom! The ceiling fell in knocking over all the surgeons and nurses. Then, scarcely a moment later, the door flew off its hinges and the rabbits marched in, attired in combat fatigues that caused me to flash back to Arnold Schwarzenegger in *Commando*. They grabbed my gurney and pushed it out of the operating room, down the hall, and straight into their submarine. What was their submarine doing on the fifth floor of the hospital? Then, as

Commander Zeko started up the engine, Sacher released me from my bonds and I was once again able to move my limbs.

"Man, those brain surgeons are trouble," I observed.

"It's not over yet," Sacher cautioned. "They're following us."

Sure enough, as the rabbits' submarine sped out of the Medical Facility, we noticed, on our electronic monitors, that the brain surgeons had boarded a giant mobile road drill and were pursuing us at full speed. The rabbits' submarine emerged from the turreted hospital in a flash and then submerged more or less through the street. I can't explain exactly how they did it. Under ordinary circumstances we would have been free of any pursuer of course, but the brain surgeons had a road drill, and it soon proved to be quite adaptable as a mobile *underground* road drill. We drove forward at amazing speed, but they hurtled toward us, forcing their way through the rocks and cement that we traversed as if sliding on silk.

Commander Zeko looked quite intense. Sacher was calm, however, puffing a large pink cigar that sent out wafts of lavender-scent. Zeko pulled a blue lever, and we suddenly found ourselves inside a volcano, viewing the lava through the glass paneling. "There's no way the brain surgeons can follow us here," I mused.

"Let's see," said Sacher sagaciously.

In fact, the brain surgeons managed to cross the interdimensional barrier and were soon in lava with us. For a moment I thought I was hearing Marlene Dietrich singing that old refrain, 'Falling in lava again.' Commander Zeko pushed several red and green buttons on the control switch, pushed the blue lever forward, and pulled a large yellow switch, above her head, toward herself. "We'll try another dimension," Sacher explained, as the rabbits' submarine suddenly found itself in interplanetary space.

"They won't be able to escape the earth's gravity field," I declared, as if I had any idea what I was talking about.

But moments later, the brain surgeons showed up on our starboard. They were catching up with us.

"Their mobile underground road drill has been adapted for interplanetary travel," noted Sacher insightfully.

The surgeons' road drill was sleek and elongated; its passenger section featured porthole-style windows. Pilot and navigator sat at the front operating the drill that projected from the nose of the craft. The drill vehicle had evidently been acquired originally by the Brain Surgeons' Union of South America, and the sides of the drill vehicle were emblazoned with the initials of this organization.

The surgeons were no peace-loving citizens; they were, on the contrary, intent on trouble, and steered their drill toward us. Before we knew it, they were starting to drill a hole into the rabbits' submarine.

"Help, help," I shouted frantically.

"Relax. We have a couple of more tricks up our sleeve," Commander Zeko declared now, looking confident despite the desperation of the situation.

The submarine made the strangest noise, whirring and wailing, sounding, for a moment, rather like a banshee. But Sacher was busy rummaging through a rather roomy "closet" -- if that is what it was -- on board their sub, and finally emerged with what looked like a formidable weapon of some sort. "Zeko," said Sacher, as she hauled this gun out, "don't you think it's time we used the psychotronic ray on them."

"It's just in the experimental stages, Sacher," Zeko pointed out.

"But we've had some good results testing the weapon on dandelions," Sacher pointed out. Evidently they did not believe in testing weapons on animals.

"So what is it? What is it?" I asked impatiently.

"It's psychological warfare," Sacher informed me, as she readied the gun for use. "Our ship is fitted with aluminum deflectors which can target mind control rays on selected subjects. The gun has three settings: singing, dancing, and singing-and-dancing. I am setting it to singing-and-dancing, the most potent setting. Once I have opened fire on their ship, all of them, I mean all the brain surgeons, will have an irresistible urge to sing and dance, and will continue to sing and dance, compulsively, for about 36 hours. They will be so absorbed in singing and dancing, that they will give up the chase."

By this point, the bore of the brain surgeons' drill was penetrating into our chamber, but Sacher seemed the very epitome of serenity, evidently tranquil in the knowledge that their close proximity would only make the surgeons easier targets. So, even as their bore whirred around a few feet from our faces, Sacher aimed her psychotronic gun at the surgeons' vessel and, presto, the surgeons immediately launched into a lively rendition of "Dancing Cheek to Cheek". Ah, memories of Fred Astaire and Ginger Rogers. The surgeons were even dancing with each other, as we could see on our sub monitor.

Zeko was intently steering the sub. So Sacher had to attend to repairs. It had appeared to me that the damage must surely be serious, but after handily flicking the bore out of our sub, Sacher brought out a can of -- well, actually I don't know what it was, maybe some sort of magical paste -- dipped a large brush into the can, and painted the hole with this paste. And before I could say "Café Bombshell," the sub was sealed, the damage fixed, and no trace remained of the surgeons' vicious and unprovoked attack.

I had always wondered about the rabbits' claims to have harpists on board their submarine. You can imagine my delight when they brought out four lemur-harpists who began to perform, for our listening pleasure, the musical delights of J. B. Krumpholz and Frederick Delius.

As Sacher and I lay there, reclining on enormous satin cushions, I could not help thinking how fortunate we were to have two such talented rabbits in our household. I looked toward the captain's seat: Commander Zeko in control. I don't remember when I had last had a trip like this one.

We docked in the underground port below our apartment, and then took an elevator I had never noticed before, which let us out in the kitchen itself. "Kris, we're back," I said in triumph.

"Fine, fine," Kris replied obliviously, "help me with the cupboard, would you, Bill darling? The dishes need straightening."

21

Settin' Off a Blast!

"**W**haddya mean, we're going home? We *are* home." Sacher said, scowling as she hurled this question at me. She looked more agitated than I had ever seen her before. "We *are* home," she repeated, underlining this point with what looked like a snarl.

"Sacher, I've never seen you like this before. You are always so calm," I muttered in some surprise.

"OK, enough of this, come clean," -- that was Zeko speaking, of course. "What's the plot?"

"My research grant is over," I explained. "I was only given a grant for 10 months in Sapporo, and now it's over. We're been here 10 months already. Have you forgotten?"

"I don't believe this," Sacher said rather dismissively. "This is a pretty lame excuse. We arranged with our superiors to be transferred here, and this is our assignment. You're telling us that we have to arrange to be transferred *back* to Seattle? And here we have been such loyal companions, always here for you, waiting for you on your bedpillow. Except when we're down at the Club or riding in our platinum-plated submarine, of course. We even rescued you from the clutches of the nefarious brain surgeons. And what do we get?"

"We get stabbed in the back! That's what!" said Zeko angrily.

"We just managed to get a special highway interchange built, to give potential customers easy access to Café Bombshell! And our café is really the perfect front for our ecological work."

"Do you know how many little 'gifts' we had to make to local and national politicians to work out this deal, so that they would see its natural advantages?" Zeko asked, still incredulous.

"Didn't you notice all the boxes we've been sending?" Kris asked the rabbits.

"We just figured you were sending explosives to your friends," Sacher mused.

"Or to your enemies," Zeko added helpfully.

"Not anything serious. I mean, we send explosives internationally all the time," Sacher continued. "So why shouldn't you?"

"Well, we've been sending our belongings home," Kris explained.

"I thought you two were filing reports on us," I pointed out. "They can't be very useful reports if you couldn't even figure out something as obvious as this."

"Oh, a cruel blow," Sacher said, with a mock wince. "We've been chasing down dangerous polluters and brain surgeons and saving the world from violence and nastiness, and even running a night club on the side where, I might mention, we have been turning quite a profit. And you want to find fault..."

"I'm not finding fault, Sacher. You know that Kris and I love you both. But now it's time to pack and leave."

"Not before we finish certain business here in Japan," Sacher replied firmly. "Arrange for a one-month extension."

"Arrange for a one-month extension?!?!" Kris and I exclaimed in astonishment.

"Sure," Sacher said, "that's a fair compromise. And it will give us time to take care of some loose ends."

I decided to drop a hint to certain colleagues at the Slavic Research Center, Hokkaido University, and see what would happen. Before I knew it, a one-month visit to Tokyo Metropolitan University, on the western fringe of metropolitan Tokyo was somehow arranged. I knew the rabbits had somehow arranged this, but I thought it would be improper to mention this to my colleagues. So I kept a delicate silence.

From here out, things were more or less out of our hands. The rabbits had some business in Nagoya first, and so it was arranged that we would visit in Nagoya for a week, and from there we took a train to Tokyo. Neither Nagoya nor Tokyo was our idea; these destinations were chosen by the rabbits for reasons that I soon learned.

In Nagoya, the rabbits shunted us off to look at Nagoya Castle, with its pulchritudinous gardens, its magical tea potions, and its swan-inhabited lake. Kris and I enjoyed the garden tour. We even took Astrolabe and Sextant with us, although they didn't seem to enjoy the castle as much as we did. The cats were also a bit troubled by the size of the swans. They knew they were outclassed. Kris and I enjoyed a lunch of octopus sushi with miso soup and a glass of sake. We wrote postcards to friends in America. We bought some balloons and lost them somewhere in the garden. We even rented a tandem bicycle and rode around cherry blossom row along the south end of the park. We had a glorious time. As we learned when we returned to the hotel that evening, so too did the rabbits. Indeed, the news of their exploits was all over the Japanese media. "Magical Rabbits Put up No-Smoking Signs in Arc of Splendour Pachinko Palaces in downtown Nagoya," "Brain surgeons rounded up by Stuffed Rabbits," "Travel brochures to mysterious planet appear all over Nagoya," and "Rabbits put up anti-pollution posters, pledge to fight pollution."

We feared that all of this media coverage might complicate our lives, but it was too late to do anything about that. We decided to distract ourselves by visiting the Nagoya Postal Museum, the Shiboya Museum of Rare Butterflies, the Owari Museum of Shinto, the Daimyo Museum of Footwear, and the Shinjuku Museum of Porcelain. We also enjoyed serene strolls along the quay and through the shopping district. At the end of a week in Nagoya, during which time the headlines told a frenzied tale of mass conversion of polluting enterprises and brain surgery clinics to chocolate factories, the rabbits announced that they had finished their business in Nagoya and we could now move on to Tokyo.

When we arrived in Tokyo, the rabbits regaled us with sonorous tales of the Daimyo Clock Museum, the Museum of Gas, the National Museum of Art, the Subway Museum, the Furniture Museum, the Asukayama Park, the Honmoku Civic Park, the Atago jinja shrine, the National Diet Library, the Nihon Museum of Calligraphy, the Tamateck Amusement Park, Tokyo Summerland, the Akigawabashi Riverbed Park, and on and on and on. At first Kris and I resisted the many touristic temptations that Tokyo had to offer. We insisted on following the rabbits. But after a day of watching them clear office-workers and factory-workers out of their facilities, on 20 minutes' notice, followed by the "voluntary closures" of the polluting facilities in Suginami-ku, Nakano-ku, Nerima-ku, Musashino-shi, and Mitaka-shi districts, we decided that enough was enough. By day's end, we had had our fill of masses of people standing outside their facilities eating chocolates, grinning vapidly while their facilities were being blown up and pledging, "We're not going to be able to pollute any more," and above all, enough of trying, time and time again, to talk some sense into the rabbits.

"What do you mean *sense*?!" Zeko exclaimed during a demolition in Mitaka-shi. "Do you really think it makes sense to pollute the planet to death? Come on, let's get realistic."

It was toward the end of that rather exciting day that Kris and I heard the rabbits burst into what must be their theme song, right after converting a highly pollutant oil refinery into a chocolate factory. The song was sung to the tune of Irving Berlin's "Puttin' on the Ritz", but the rabbits had come up with their own lyrics. If I remember the lyrics correctly, they went something like this:

"Have you seen the well to do
Up and down Nakano-ku,
On that famous thoroughfare
Spewing sulfides in the air.
Smokestacks and nitrous oxides,
Discharge sulphur dioxides,
Wrecking every stream
while the animals scream.

So if you want to help to save
the earth, why don't you join us and
Make it last, by
Setting off a blast!

Different types of factories
All do their bit to rack the seas,
They all pollute.
Give 'em all the boot!

Dressed up in their fancy duds and dresses,
They don't care about their sundry messes.
No one guesses:
Come let's go with dynamite; we can move fast
And blow them up,
Right in their midst,
Giving them a fix!"

As the rabbits sang the last refrain, I looked at Kris and saw that the song was bringing back memories of her old days with the Resistance. Perhaps their revolutionary songs were similar.

At any rate, after this, we simply gave up. It was clear that the rabbits had their agenda, and we were not about to change their minds. So, with nothing else to do, we decided to just have a good time, and we spent the rest of our days in Tokyo visiting various touristic sights, making sure to check with the rabbits the night before to make sure that we would be touristing as far away from their targets as possible. What we couldn't figure out was why the rabbits were meeting so little resistance. I mean, these rabbits were blowing up major industrial plants and stopping not just pollution but production – or was I missing something? And how did chocolate figure in their activities?

22

Going Home

After a week in Nagoya and a full month in Tokyo, we had expected the rabbits to be happy to leave. Happy was not the word. Reconciled, perhaps, but still full of complaints. But at least we were moving beyond mere objections to discussions of alternative front organizations for the rabbits' work.

"It's not fair," Zeko pouted. "What about our platinum-plated submarine? What about our Café? What about all the politicians we have in our pocket?"

"Why don't you open another Café Bombshell in Seattle," Kris suggested. "After all, Café Bombshell should go world-wide, shouldn't it?"

"Well, maybe," said Sacher with a curious look on her face.

"Or maybe you two could open a language school. That would make a good front organization. And how many languages do you know between the two of you? --German, Italian, Korean, Arabic, Portuguese, Japanese, Twi, anything else?"

"We know some Norwegian," said Zeko, "and also a few words of Xyponese that we picked up on Planet Xypon. We brought back a complete set of books and CDs, on *How to Speak Xyponese*. I think we could get to the point where we could teach Xyponese too. You may be right: that could serve as an ideal front for our activities, while enabling us, in hiring our teachers, to continue to recruit comrades to the cause."

"Of course, there's not likely to be a big demand for Xyponese on Planet Earth," I pointed out.

"No, not a language school," said Sacher thoughtfully. "We're night-club owners."

"And eco-terrorists," Zeko added.

"How about opening a school in how to operate a submarine?" Kris offered.

"Oh, big demand there," commented Zeko, dismissively. "Humans prefer cars and bicycles, at least around the city. Only higher species like rabbits appreciate the wonders of inner-city submarine travel."

"Oh scum!" Sacher muttered, in what sounded to me like some sort of leftist curse. There were a few moments of silence and then Sacher said, "We're not flying in the baggage this time. We want to be in the coach with everyone else."

"Hey, why don't you two buy your own tickets if you're so well funded? The government should pick up the tab, no?"

"Why bother," came Zeko's inevitable reply. "When the stewardess comes by, we'll just do our stuffed animal imitations. It's never failed. And besides, if we went off and rode first class, who would tell you two what to do?"

The rabbits then told us that if we agreed to let them sit on our laps on the flight back, they would make the flight arrangements for us and save us a lot of money. We should have known better, but, of course, we didn't. So we agreed to their suggestion. The rabbits arranged for Astrolabe and Sexy to be flown to the U.S. by some sort of Pet Transfer Service. Neither Kris nor I had ever heard of the service, but we took it on good faith that it was a legitimate business. After all, it had our stuffed rabbits' recommendation. As for our own transportation home, I did think it was a little odd that instead of flying out of Sapporo International Airport, we had reservations flying out of Sapporo Air Station, and that instead of flying direct to Seattle, or at least to Los Angeles, we were flying to Guam, and transferring planes there.

Our flight out of Sapporo Air Station was a "hopper". There were a lot of people in uniforms on our flight, but after all, people in uniforms are allowed on planes too. It's not exactly the same as being, well, naked or something. But Kris and I grew more suspicious when we saw we were landing in Guam and at Guam Air Base, USAF, at that. "Oh, this looks promising," I caught myself muttering to myself as I read the sign from the small porthole that passed for a window.

It turned out that the rabbits had arranged for us to fly on a military carrier, along with various air force personnel, from Guam Air Base back to Makah Air Station on the Olympic Peninsula. It was to be an inspiring flight. We were not at all surprised, by this point, to find that we were the only persons not in uniform on the entire flight, or to see that all the other passengers were hauling in huge khaki duffel bags and shoving them into storage spaces that were meant for baggage about half the size. Then, as the flight got underway, the chief stewardess came out, and began her routine:

"Good morning airmen and guests, we are about to take off shortly for Makah Air Base. My name is Lieutenant Pilsudska, and I would like to welcome you on board. Pay attention now as we explain a few safety features of this aircraft. Follow along in the *Airman's Guide to Operational Safety*, which you will remove from the seatpocket in front of you." I could not help noticing that the lieutenant was giving us orders, not suggestions.

"Our aircraft is equipped with six emergency doors," the lieutenant continued, "which are used in the event of emergencies, and fire extinguishing equipment, which is used in the event of fire, and parachutes, which are used in the event that the aircraft explodes or is shot down by international terrorists.

"Your seat-back is convertible into a flotation device, and also contains, in the zippered pocket on each side, a three-week supply of high-nutrition pills and flasks of enriched apple cider, to sustain you during the time that the search party is searching for you. The plane is also equipped with sirens and large flashing red lights above each seat. In the event of an emergency, the sirens will wail and the large flashing red lights will flash.

"Under your seat, you will find your own personal parachute. Please put on your parachute now, placing your head through the looping hitch. Put your arms under the side straps, pulling the red strap until the parachute is tight and snug. In the event that this aircraft is shot down by international terrorists, the floor under your seat will open up and your seat will fall through the hatch. In that event, you should count to five and then pull the green cord to your parachute. Do not pull the blue cord as this will release all straps and cause the parachute to fly away from your body.

"This is a no-smoking flight. Passengers are permitted to chew tobacco in designated tobacco-chewing aisles, but are reminded that all masticated tobacco should be deposited in the spittoons provided for this purpose.

"Our captain today is Major John Lark. Our navigator is Captain Freddy Friedenhofer. Other members of our cabin crew are Sergeant Starac, Airman Pipper, and Airman Fireball. Cabin crew, prepare now for takeoff."

The rabbits were in full agreement with the concerns about tobacco pollution but they felt that the briefing should not have condemned all terrorists without making some distinctions. They thought that the briefing should have included some credit to eco-terrorists for fighting to save the planet. In fact, they continued to grumble about this and wouldn't stop. At first I tried humming to block out their incessant grumbling. But I soon stopped listening to the rabbits altogether, and was fascinated to see the cabin crew passing each other in the aisles, because every time one of the enlisted crew passed the lieutenant, the enlisted man had to salute the lieutenant, who then had to return the salute. After the eighth or ninth time, it started to seem more like a puppet show than an airline.

Then came the meal: high nutrition enriched wheat toast, a patty that must have been meat (although I could not be sure), a small bar labeled "USAF Chocolate: Approved by the Secretary of Defense for Consumption on all USAF Flights," a small can of tomato juice, and a small dish of lime jello. Next to this "USAF-approved" meal was a package. On the side panel, in small letters, one could read, "Anti-regurgitation pills. Take two pills at the start of our flight in order to reduce the proclivity to regurgitate."

But the best part was the film. I always like airplane films, above all because there is very little else to do but also because, if you don't like the soundtrack, all you need to do is take off the earphones. I did read once about an airline that offered shuffle-board in the first-class section, but that was a rare find. It also was a welcome surprise to find that the Air Force was not charging us for the headsets. The film was actually free of charge!

As the film started, I became aware that the film showed the American flag fluttering and that our national anthem was playing. All the passengers undid their seatbelts and rose for the national anthem. It was an inspiring scene. Then, as the anthem ended and we took our seats once more, the feature film began: "Your Future in the US Air Force," with General Mervin M. Mervin, narrator. Naturally, it was just as this film reached the most rivetting part, when my muscles were taut with intense excitement, that the captain came over the loud-speaker.

"Hello airmen, this is your captain speaking, although actually I'm a major, not a captain. The navigator is a captain, but I'm a major. That's why I'm in charge on this flight and he isn't. So I'm not really a captain at all....Ahem, this is your major speaking, Major John Lark, commander of this flight. We are currently flying at an altitude of 50,000 feet. Actually that is not exactly correct, we are actually flying at an altitude of 47,000 feet, but we are gaining altitude gradually, and will probably be at an altitude of 50,000 feet pretty soon, maybe even 52,000 feet. If you look to the left you will see the Air Force Station at Unalaska. In about 15 minutes, we will be passing over Kodiak Air Base, on Kodiak Island. I will period-ically check back with you to point out additional USAF sites of interest. Let me just remind you to keep your parachute fastened, just in case our aircraft is downed. This is Major Lark signing off."

As he signed off, all the cabin staff stood erect and salut-ed.

The film ended with a rousing rendition of "Off We Go into the Wild Blue Yonder." I could see that the airmen were deeply inspired by the film, even awed. It was a happy sight. Meanwhile, now that the film was over, the rabbits began to chatter. To begin with, they loved the view. They behaved as if they had never been on a plane before and kept comparing what it is like to be flying above the clouds to riding *on* the clouds. But suddenly there was a beep from Zeko's wristwatch and a coded message began paging down its face. It was headquarters. I looked over Zeko's shoulder to read the message, which read, "Omecay mediatelyimay otay Evadanay. Eway avehay naay ergencyemay niay Aslay Egasvay." Good thing I worked so hard in Latin class back in high school, because I immediately figured out that this meant trouble in Las Vegas.

23

Saving the Planet in Las Vegas

We had heard about the Fat One before. But until we arrived in Las Vegas we did not know his real name – Huey Looey; apparently he was named after two of Donald Duck's nephews! After all, he had been working as a parking attendant at one of the fancier hotels in Las Vegas, and you just don't read much about parking attendants in the press. In those days no one called him the Fat One, even though he already weighed 480 pounds; they just called him Huey. Or sometimes, "Hey you, lunatic!" But Huey was also a gambler, losing about half of his wages in black jack every payday for years on end. But one day Huey's luck turned and he became fabulously rich. He immediately drove to a Crano-Gas therapeutic and fuel facility and requested a 'makeover.'

Crano-Gas offers four alternative 'makeovers': very happy, extremely happy, ecstatically happy, and insanely happy. You wouldn't think that anything with the word 'insane' in it would be very popular, but, in fact, that was their best-selling 'makeover'. At any rate, Huey was fed up being bored and asked for 'insanely happy'. From the pictures of him I saw on the television later, I don't think he looked so happy – he did look insane, however, with his mouth frozen into a strange post-surgical smile. But right after the brain surgery, Huey bought some new clothes, quit his job as parking attendant, and moved to Afghanistan, where he opened a take-in laundry and brain surgery clinic. I understand that in those days he was known as Ahmad Ben-Huey Looey. But the laundry was only a front organization designed to conceal his real purpose, which was to join the mujaheddin and wage a war of revenge against the entire Western world, which he blamed as a whole for the materialistic messages in Western popular culture and for the boring work of parking attendants. He also was part of the international brain surgery conspiracy, and soon became its leading figure. Before long, he had some 3,000 'laundry operatives' working for him; most of them never washed a single shirt. But they performed a lot of lobotomies.

Then, one day, Huey told his operatives that from that day forward they should call him the Fat One. He also started to wear hideous sparkle bow-ties and red rubber shirts and pants. It was a moment which might have been taken from Mickiewicz's epic tales. With his new name and new rubber attire, the Fat One seemed to become more dangerous than ever. He now hatched a plot to strike at Las Vegas. His idea was to fire shells containing high concentrates of poisonous ethyl acrylate, into the largest casinos in downtown Las Vegas, an action which was designed to induce sore eyes, headache, vomiting, breathing problems, choking, and high fever, as a first step toward the destruction of the Western world as we know it. Some 283 of his 'laundry operatives' put on black ski masks and hired a fleet of fork lift trucks in Los Angeles and drove them to Las Vegas, loaded with this dangerous cargo. Police soon picked up the fleet on aerial surveillance but were confused. They apparently assumed that these were just ordinary members of the working class, no doubt heading to a convention of fork lift truck operators somewhere in Nevada. The police took no precautions at all, in fact. But when the 283 'laundry operatives' arrived at Las Vegas city limits, they began to sing something about Sodom and Gomorrah to the tune of "Happy Days Are Here Again". Police sergeant Marvin Roy Metrick heard this and radioed in to headquarters. But the chief thought it was just some sort of a joke, so he ignored it. Probably just some sort of religious event.

Then it happened. The operatives started to ram the cars off the road, and then made for the hotels. In some cases, they drove straight into the hotels, shouting "Down with American imperialism!" and began to cause a great deal of destruction. In other cases, they simply rammed the hotels. There were explosions and fires and pretty soon the whole town was in chaos. They also started to fire their high pollutant shells into the casinos. People were screaming and rubbing their eyes. The operatives now tried to escape, having forgotten that fork lift trucks are not capable of high speeds. Eventually, about 40 of them were rounded up and put in jail. The remaining 243 remained at large.

The governor of Nevada went on television, declaring a state of emergency. But his broadcast was interrupted by some jamming broadcast in which the remaining 'laundry operatives' listed their demands. They demanded that the governor resign (to be replaced by the Fat One), that the sum of $20 billion be deposited to the account of the International Brain Surgery Conspiracy, that all anti-pollution laws in the state of Nevada be declared null and void, and that any anti-smoking ordinances in the state of Nevada be immediately rescinded. The Fat One also came on screen and announced that he had taken the owners of four of the larger casinos as hostages, and would execute them if his demands were not met. He then put the four owners on screen where they were forced to engage in ritual self-criticism, and then five 'laundry operatives' came on screen to sing a few stanzas of "The whole world's an ashtray" to the tune of "St. James' Infermary", it went something like this:

The whole world's an ashtray
I spread my ash around,
I stick my butt into the ground
Man, that sure feels good.

When I chew gum and when I'm done
I spit it on the street
And when there's gum between my feet,
Man, that sure feels neat.

And when I feel saliva
buildin' up inside my mouth,
I know there's one solution:
gotta gotta spit it out.

The whole world's an ashtray –
cigarette butts and gum and spit,
and when you stop and think about it,
Man, that sure feels good.

The rabbits arrived in Las Vegas, with us in tow, the same evening and we immediately contacted the governor at his Las Vegas office. (Carson City may be the capital, but Las Vegas is the pulsing heart of the state of Nevada.) The governor graciously allowed Kris and me into his office, since we were the rabbits' caretakers, but it was clear that his business was with the rabbits, not with us. We were given some chocolates

and coffee, and were expected to enjoy these victuals in silence. The governor explained the situation to the rabbits, and
I will admit that it seemed very complicated. I gazed out the
window, and there, hovering in the sky, I spied an enormous
extraterrestrial craft. Its engine made a sound much like the
town ice cream wagon, but no one else noticed it. And no one
else seemed ·to notice when whoever was on board started
to shout, through a megaphone, "Your brain must come out
now! Your brain is next! Yes, we mean you. Your brain is next!"
I shut my eyes tight and held my breath, and hoped that the
craft would go away.

The governor was, evidently, a sensible man, because he
quickly decided to give the rabbits full authority in the state
of Nevada until the brain surgeons/fork lift truck operators
had been routed. The rabbits had repeatedly found solutions
in music – with their Italian opera, with their psychotronic
ray, and, most recently, with their song about Nagano-ku. As
green anarchists, they remained committed to a nonviolent
struggle: destroy pollutant factories but do not harm people
or animals. Polluters must be reeducated, not liquidated. Brain
surgeons must be rehabilitated, not decapitated. So, Sacher
argued, the first step in the struggle was to write a good song.
Zeko was not so sure about this and thought that setting off
some explosives might be a better way to start. But Sacher's
moderation prevailed and after several false starts, they came
up with the following song,

> *Pollution is bad, it rots the brain,*
> *Toxic waste makes you insane,*
> *If you breathe in all that waste*
> *And you don't know the stuff with which it's laced,*
> *You could rot or crash or die,*
> *Your body floating in the sky,*
> *You could lose your teeth and thumb,*
> *Join the resistance and don't be dumb!*

Surgeons like their work just fine,
Cutting patients is sublime.
But lobotomies are not so great,
Air-heads shouldn't be our fate.
Stop the surgeons while we can,
Let's impose a lobotomy ban!
End the conspiracy, sing a song,
We'll save the planet before too long.

The rabbits called in their troupe of robotic weasels, who numbered about 120, and set this song to a heavy metal beat. They orchestrated it for electric guitars, electric harmonicas, electric guslas, drums, amplified hairpins, and psychedelic sackbutts, and rocked their way up Las Vegas Boulevard.

The Fat One and his fork lift truck operators had taken control of four of Las Vegas' leading hotels: Caesar's Palace, the Golden Nugget with its Victorian refinement, the Riviera, and, of course, the Stardust. Rumors were that the Fat One had set up camp in a secret luxury suite in a secret wing of the Riviera, close to its 120,000 square foot casino. There were also rumors that the room was soundproof – rumors which, if true, could have spelled trouble for the rabbits' plan. Besides, what if the conspirators were tone deaf?!?

Indeed, as the rabbits and weasels rocked their way up the boulevard, things did not seem to go well. The fork-lift truck operators hurled canisters full of pollutants at the parade and shouted curses such as "Down with clean air! Stop thinking for yourselves! Thinking is bad! Down with music! Don't give us facts! Give us pollution!" The parade beat a retreat to The Flamingo, where the rabbits had set up headquarters. Here, ensconced in their luxury suite, the rabbits took counsel from the weasels, and considered their alternatives. Zeko's first thought was to strike Las Vegas Bridge with missiles, but the clever weasels, programmed with vast megabytes of information, quickly pointed out that Las Vegas Bridge is a card game and not an architectural feature. Inevitably I pointed out that I had seen an extraterrestrial spacecraft through the window at the governor's mansion, and I was very pleased to see that this information was taken very seriously.

"It could be the Teronese," suggested Zeko, "working in tandem with the international brain surgery conspiracy."

"Or it could be intelligence units from some other planet," Sacher cautioned.

Brian, the weasel, whose name is an anagram for "brain" and who knew an awful lot about brains and extraterrestrials, as well as about the brains and thought processes of extraterrestrials, offered some reflections. "If they are the Teronese," Brian said, "then they are going to come in force. These are not the sort of extraterrestrials to piddle around. There will be lots of them, flying in lots of different craft. But there are two characteristics of theirs that we can exploit. The first is that they cannot stand bright light. The second is that every Teronian has two brains – "

"Hold on!!" I blurted out. "Two brains? Are you sure?"

"Well, look," said Brian, "you have a cerebrum, a cerebellum, and a medulla oblongata, working in harmony. What if one of them 'seceded' and set itself up as an independent brain, working separately from the others? What if the cerebellum, for example, went its own way? Then you would have two brains."

"Uh huh…"

"That's what happened with the Teronese," Brian continued. "Life on Planet Teron evolved much like on earth, except that while, on earth, we think that we have the survival of the fittest, on Teron that was not necessarily so. The one-brainers died out many millions of years ago, and only the two-brainers survived, apparently because, with two brains, these creatures had twice the sexual interest and were having sex twice as often as the one-brainers. Moreover, since there is no information loop between one brain and the other, one brain might not even be aware when the other brain is enjoying sexual pleasure. So that brain remains hungry for sex."

"But there is only one body."

"Right, one body, two brains. It is very interesting."

"OK, Brian," Zeko said, "let's cut to the chase. How are we going to exploit these peculiarities for our purposes?"

"Well, assuming that there are, in fact, Teronese attacking us here on Planet Earth," Brian replied, "we could light up Las Vegas as it has never been lit up before, and then use radio waves to send contradictory messages, beaming it straight at their spaceships. This would probably do the trick."

"OK," Zeko said, "but contradictory messages about what? What they like and what they hate?"

Fortunately, Sacher had read more about Planet Teron than Zeko had, and knew that the Teronese were an advanced species of moss, basically two-brained moss creatures, who therefore liked water, shade, and rocks but hated sand and direct sunlight. Apparently, they also hated bleach, which hurt these delicate flora. They also hated listening to political speeches.

The rabbits now placed a call to their friends on Planet Xypon to get more information, and to confirm that our planet was, indeed, under attack. The Xyponese confirmed our suspicions but were not in a position to come to our rescue. However, they did offer to declare a quarantine zone around Planet Teron, and not allow anyone else to leave that planet. That was at least *something*. Meanwhile, the weasels began preparations for an assault which would involve light reflectors and lots of sand and political speeches. The weasels worked late into the night and, as night closed in on us, like a team of brain surgeons, I pulled the blanket over my eyes and tried to get some sleep.

In the morning, it was the Fat One's show. At first it was quiet enough, as quiet as Las Vegas has ever been at 9 a.m.

Then, at the Riviera, a giant golden turnip rose out of the ground at the stroke of 9, and there, standing in the middle, amid a circle of small fountains was the Fat One, decked out in his red rubber suit, complete with yellow rubber cape. He was puffing on an enormous cigar and grinning so broadly that his lips nearly touched his nostrils. As he stood there, blue mist arose around the turnip and then six curvaceous beauties popped out of the golden turnip and gathered around him. He had a microphone around his neck and now spoke:

"Good morning fans and future fans. This is the Fat One wishing you a great morning. Say good morning to my lovely ladies – Amyjoy, Lucijoy, Julijoy, Jillyjoy, Debbiejoy, and Marcijoy." They wiggled and there were shouts of approval from the fork-lift truck operators, some of them with tell-tale scars just about the eyebrows, who were swarming around the golden turnip. "Yes, today is an important day, because today, I am taking over the planet. And say hello to the riders in the sky!" And they were right on cue, because, just that minute, a vast swarm of Teronese space vehicles appeared in the distance.

The rabbits were picking up their conversations on radar, and, from what I could hear, it appeared that every Teronian moss unit was arguing with itself, with one brain having one opinion and the other brain having a contrary opinion. But their craft were armed with missiles, I guessed, and we might all be in great danger. The rabbits, however, were prepared for this eventuality and ordered the weasels to beam radio transmissions to the Teronese space vehicles. Apparently, the brains picked up different frequencies, so that it was possible, by beaming contradictory messages at two alternative frequencies, to feed contradictory messages to the two brains of each Teronian. Thanks to the high technology which the rabbits and weasels had developed, we were able to listen to their conversations with themselves and hear the arguments which ensued.

"The rabbits' headquarters is five miles to the West," the first Teronian began. "No it isn't, it's ten miles to the East. No it isn't, it's to the West. We should aim our missiles dead center at their headquarters. No, we should strike at the dam. No, the headquarters. No, the dam." And that was just one of the two-brained moss creatures arguing with itself.

Eventually, the arguing became so intense that their craft, hundreds of them, were just zig-zagging around in confusion, as first one brain and then the other would take control of the craft. At this point, the rabbits switched to phase two, which involved bright lights and political speeches. All of us donned our sunglasses as the weasels started to beam up political speeches from local congressional districts. I was nervous about this, but Kris seemed pretty confident that the Teronese would find these speeches as boring as she did. She was sure that the combination of bright light and boring speeches would be too much for the Teronese, just as the rabbits had predicted, and she was right. After a short while, the Teronese flew out of there as fast as they could. As they flew away, I thought I heard them sing,

It's been a lousy lousy day
And we came from far away,
But those speeches are inane,
And they're driving us insane,
And we wish we hadn't come
Cause we're starting to feel numb,
And it's time we headed home
To our moisture, rock, and loam.

And with that, they were gone. But the Fat One was not about to give up. After all, he still had 243 laundry operatives driving fork-lift trucks at his command, and he had rubber outfits, and he had hostages, and he had control of four of Las Vegas' best hotels. The weasel-commandoes were ready for action, however, having been trained not only to wait tables, analyze complex problems, play musical instruments, and operate advanced technological gear, but also to serve as an elite police squad capable of setting up a siege or even ending it. They were wearing fine black uniforms which looked a lot more sensible than the red rubberwear favored by the Fat One, or, for that matter, the lime green frolic-wear favored by his laundry operatives. I figured that on fashion grounds alone, the weasels had already won the day.

But the Fat One was not about to submit his demands to an independent jury who would judge his case on the basis of fashion. He and his ladies had retreated back into the Riviera and, with 2,075 rooms and suites, not to mention the enormous casino area, the Riviera offered many places for the Fat One to hide. But again, there was a simple solution. The weasels sealed the hotel and then set up pumps at various positions around the hotel. Then, just before entering the hotel in force, they donned gas masks and then turned on the pumps to pump in a stable mixture of nitrogen oxide, dinitrogen monoxide, hyponitrous acid anhydride, and facticious air, known as nitrous oxide or, more colloquially, laughing gas. Discovered by English scientist Joseph Priestly in 1793, the gas was initially used by the English in order to assist them in getting over the loss of their American colonies, but later came to be used primarily for recreational purposes. However, our clever rabbits and weasels realized that laughing gas, which induces both merriment and massive confusion in those who inhale it, could be a powerful anti-terrorist weapon.

We remained, of course, at a safe distance and did not witness the assault on the Riviera at close range. But from the stories we heard later, we understand that the weasels burst into the Riviera to find the sounds of laughter reverberating throughout the hotel, but especially from the main floor, where many of the laundry operatives were trying to hide behind some of the 1,400 slot machines in the casino, while

The weasels donned gas masks and started pumping in laughing gas.

laughing hysterically. They were laughing so hard that they could not even stand up, let alone hold or operate their weapons. The weasels easily took them into custody and then began to search for the Fat One and his hostages, following the sounds of laughter up to the 8th floor.

"Don't come any closer, ha-ha-ha," warned the Fat One as if it were some hilarious joke. "If you come any closer, ha-ha-ha, I'll blow out their brains, ha-ha-ha." It was, apparently, hard to take the threat seriously, with all of the laughter, not to mention the fact that the Fat One was sitting on a pile of silk cushions, literally writhing and shaking with merriment. It was an easy matter to take him into custody, to free the hostages, and to end this drama.

The Fat One was sent to prison, where he was assigned to park the cars of the guards. The laundry operatives were delivered into the custody of the rabbits for reprogramming. The governor was hailed by the people of Nevada and the world, and reelected to office. And the rabbits came back to Seattle with us to continue to operate their cafés and fight for justice. But what about the international brain surgery conspiracy? Had it been vanquished for good, or was it merely going underground and waiting for better days? At that time, we did not know for sure.

THE END